A Dollop of Toothpaste

BILLY VERA

I'd like to thank my great friend Tamela D'Amico for her tireless efforts on my behalf. To Alan Swyer for his support and belief that I was on the right path. To James Austin whose painting brought Johnny and Paulette to life.

Let me tell you 'bout Ooh Poo Pah Doo.
Jessie Hill

CHAPTER ONE

September 11, 2021.

"THE CITY OF GEFFENSBORO, FORMERLY KNOWN as Los Angeles, California, is no more," said newscaster Shepard Smith from the midtown Manhattan TV studio of Fox News, in that exceedingly earnest way he had of delivering the news of the day. "Exactly twenty years ago this morning, I stood on this very spot and reported another tragedy, the first plane crashing into the World Trade Center. And now, Pentagon sources tell us, where once stood a bustling city of over nine million Americans, there lies nothing but nuclear waste."

In room 206 at the Ramada Inn in Austin, Texas, Johnny Santoro, having heard a blood-curdling scream in the next room, ran from the shower and was now standing next to the bed, covered in a towel. Dripping water on the floor, he watched the screen as the girl he'd brought back to his room after the gig the night before sat on the side of his bed, tears rolling down her young cheeks. His initial instinct was to try and comfort her, but frankly, he couldn't remember her name.

As he looked around the room, an exact replica of every other Ramada Inn room in the world, he thought of his former wife and two grown children. He thought of the house he'd bought for cash in the old school Italian manner, back when he'd been flush. He thought also of his vinyl record collection and several vintage Fender guitars. All gone now, reduced to radioactive dust.

Slowly, the gravity of his situation became more clear in his mind. What was left? All he had now was his credit card and the cash in his pocket. Those, and his recently acquired holographic iPhone. His favorite old 1959 Telecaster, along with a spare '62, and his gig amps, a vintage tweed-covered Fender Bassman and a smaller Fender Champ, were both sitting out in the parking lot, waiting to be packed onto the tour bus by the stage crew.

Born in 1956, the year Elvis Presley arrived, full-blown, on the national scene, and now, at age 65, a time when he'd once hoped to be lying on a beach somewhere in blissful retirement, Johnny still found himself playing rhythm guitar for pop music star Bonnie Raitt. But a Republican congress, who'd been unable to pass any meaningful legislation during the first two years of President Donald Trump's administration, despite the fact that they held both the House and the Senate, had finally managed only to raise the retirement age to seventy-five in a feeble attempt to keep the country from bankruptcy and keep Social Security somewhat solvent. The day after Trump signed the bill into law, MSNBC's Lawrence O'Donnell hysterically reported on a group of wheezing, harmless old Tea Partiers peacefully protesting the new law in wheel chairs and walkers, mischaracterizing the event as "a scene of Nazi fascist violence never before seen in this great nation of ours."

The Republicans' misstep led to their ouster in the 2018 mid-term election, enabling the Democrats to take over both houses and easily pass laws lowering the voting age to sixteen and granting the right to vote to any person currently residing in the United States, legal or otherwise, with or without ID, practically guaranteeing that no Republican would hold higher office for the next fifty years.

Drunk with power, the liberal Ninth Circuit Court in northern California ruled that any city with a religious-sounding name be required to change it or risk losing federal funding for violating the rule against separation of Church and State. Thus, the City of Angels was renamed Geffensboro, after the state's biggest political donor, David Geffen. San Diego was now called Puerto de la Raza. St. Paul was Princetown, after sister city Minneapolis's favorite son, the late musician. Budweiser City now stood on the piece of earth once known as St. Louis and San Francisco was renamed Leningrad after a heated city council debate decided that Pelosiville sounded too much like Palookaville.

Things only got crazier during the 2020 election cycle. A pair of out-of-work actresses, disguised in bright red "Make America *Really* Great This Time" baseball caps, somehow managed to get within feet of the president's podium and lobbed two hand grenades onto the stage, assassinating the much-loathed leader of the free world along with his vice president and his former fashion model wife in one fell swoop.

The multi-tasking Trump had been in mid-Tweet while delivering a speech from a Teleprompter, veering off script into his typically indecipherable ad lib Queens patois. Whenever he was unable to think of what to say, he had a habit of repeating himself, often several times over the course of the same sentence. His last-ever Tweet on this planet read, in part, "This election is a disaster. After the votes are counted you'll all be very sorry because I'm not POTUS anymore. Sad." The Speaker of the House, fearing for her life, remained hidden in a bunker in an undisclosed location somewhere in Montana, while unelected former Obama administration holdovers, which Republican pundits had named "the deep state," effectively ran the government, as if their former chief had never left office.

In part--and for once--Trump was correct. The race *was* a disaster, and not just for him. In the primaries, the Democrats' progressive wing had argued over whether to run 79-year old socialist Bernie Sanders or quasi-socialist Kamala Harris, with New York City mayor Bill de Blasio as her running mate. The Party's more moderate establishment wing pondered over 78-year old Joe Biden who faced an uphill battle against the still-powerful Clinton machine, which favored running former First Daughter Chelsea for her nostalgia appeal. Hillary, distracted by her new wife, Huma Abadin, seemed to have lost the fire in her belly for another run, prompting the always-provocative Ann Coulter to quip, "Don't count on it; she's like herpes, we'll never be rid of her."

For their part, the Republicans ran their usual pack of boring idiot senators, governors and political hacks in the vain hope of offsetting the public's memory of the dysfunctional Trump administration. The mainstream, moderate GOP's greatest fear was the looming prospect of a Sean Hannity candidacy. Rumor had it that they'd found a transgender Bush distant cousin, hoping to siphon off enough of the youth vote while simultaneously holding on to aging fans of the obsolete Bush dynasty. Even the most clueless Republicans had written off the Evangelicals by now, as they were no longer a serious factor in a nation that the latest polls indicated was 79% atheist.

In the midst of the fray, a publicist for the popular movie star Dwayne Johnson aka The Rock, announced he was considering a run and forming his own party, cleverly named Rock On, throwing both traditional political parties into a panic. Rush Limbaugh and Stephen Colbert both agreed for once that The Rock must be stopped at all costs. But, as he had a new blockbuster summer release in the pipeline, nobody knew for sure if he was serious or if his threat was merely a publicist's ploy to drum up sagging ticket sales.

As things turned out, The Rock siphoned off votes mainly from the Republicans, but not quite enough to win. In a surprise last minute move, the desperate Democrats decided to counter with a celebrity of their own.

The geezer contingent pitched for Bruce Springsteen, but no one under the age of 50 knew who he was. Firebrand Al Sharpton and Representative Maxine Waters demanded that rapper Jay Z be allowed to run but were largely ignored as the Party elders assumed they had the black vote locked up anyway, so why bother trying to placate them.

Everyone knew and loved The Rock, but 2020 was not the year for a centrist candidate.

Suddenly realizing they had slit their own throats by lowering the voting age and getting rid of the voter ID requirement, the Dems opted for potty mouth stand-up comic Sarah Silverman. To cover all the politically correct demographic bases, the campaign geniuses had the comedian pretend to be gay and to have suddenly "discovered" she had 6% Aztec and 4% Kenyan blood running through her veins after presenting a bogus DNA saliva test.

She gave a stump speech on the Upper West Side of Manhattan in which she claimed she was born with the genital plumbing of both "genders." With this shamelessly blatant appeal to the college kids and high schoolers, she easily laid waste to the Republicans, dashing their hopes for at least another four years, having successfully pandered to every group in the country who sophomorically saw themselves as victims of a racist and homophobic society.

Fortunately for the country, the establishment Democrats still controlled both houses, so the comedian's loopier policy ideas never had a chance of getting off the ground.

On the TV, back in room 206 at the Ramada Inn in Austin, ol' Shep Smith was still rambling on in his smooth baritone, something about how President Silverman was expected to address the nation "soon." Johnny grabbed the remote and switched over to CNN. He always liked to get both sides of the story which, for a change, were pretty much the same, as nobody knew yet from whom or from where the bomb had come. An avowed, registered Independent, he liked to call himself a "card-carrying cynic" when it came to politics, telling anyone who inquired, "I belong to no party. I think for myself," a novel concept in an age where blind, emotionalist tribalism ruled most people's thinking.

His cynicism was no surprise to those who knew his background. As a great nephew of the infamous Carlos Marcello, the Al Capone of New

Orleans, he was brought up to see first hand how politicians were put on this earth to be bought and paid for, their only interest being in getting elected, and reelected. Marcello, along with Santo Traficante of Tampa and Sam Giancana of Chicago had been behind the assassination of John Fitzgerald Kennedy in 1963. Dallas, the site of the murder, as well as all of eastern Texas, was also part of Marcello's fiefdom.

After old Papa Joe Kennedy had made a deal in 1960 with Carlos and his friends to let them run their business without interference in return for assuring his boy's election, JFK's brother Bobby double-crossed them and had the Feds kidnap Marcello and drop him in the jungle of Guatemala, the country where he'd been born of Sicilian blood.

Carlos escaped and made his way back to the Big Easy via Grand Isle. His boys asked him if he planned to kill Bobby, to which he responded, "No, you wanna kill the snake you gotta cut off the head," and so began the plot to kill the 35th President of the United States.

But the old man was long dead now and what was left of the mob was run by Johnny's 98-year old uncle Nicky.

At that moment, the phone rang and Johnny almost jumped out of his skin. Seeing the area code 504 on his screen, he was not surprised when he heard the rasp of his uncle's voice on the other end of the line.

"You watchin' the TV baby? The shit's about to go down, so drop everything and get yo' ass down here quick."

Then the TV went black.

When it came back on a few minutes later, Shepard Smith had vanished. In his place was some local anchor. She was saying something about the nation's power grid being down in the Northeastern sector, from Boston, south past Washington, D.C. and west to Chicago.

"You see that shit, man?" said Uncle Nicky, "Now get the fuck down here. We got work to do!"

CHAPTER 2

THE GIRL WAS STILL SITTING THERE, HER BRIGHT
blue eyes glued to the TV, when he returned from the meeting of the band
and stage crew. Bonnie wasn't present, having already left for her home
in upstate California, driven by her personal assistant and accompanied
by an armed bodyguard. The two tour bus drivers had been given orders
to drop her employees wherever they wished to go, which caused some
confusion, as many of them no longer had a home to return to.

Salaries and *per diems* were distributed in cash and travel plans were
made for later in the day, after an extended check-out time was arranged
with the hotel. In the afternoon, those who were headed east of the
Mississippi boarded one bus and those who had somewhere to stay in the
west were loaded onto the other.

During the meeting, Johnny had sat with Pete Holman, his guitar tech
and only close friend among the band and crew. As with many music acts
these days, the musicians seen by the audience were young, hip, good looking and "diverse," while the actual music was played by several old pros
hidden from sight off-stage. Johnny was one of this latter group.

Pete, a tall, muscular man of fifty-two and a former Navy Seal, was
from the New York City suburb of White Plains, actually Greenburgh,
the unincorporated town inhabited mostly by blacks like himself and the
descendants of the southern Italians, mainly from Calabria, Abruzzo and

Naples, who'd been brought from the old country in the early half of the previous century as stone masons to build the Kensico Dam in Valhalla and the Merritt Parkway up through Westchester and Connecticut.

When not on tour, Holman lived with his aging mother and younger sister in the wooden three-bedroom house where he'd grown up with them and his late father. His room was piled, floor to ceiling with books of every kind and description, for he had a voracious hunger for knowledge, a photographic memory and could discuss virtually any subject other than math or science, of which he had a phobia. On the road, his hobby was perusing used bookstores and second-hand shops for old paperbacks, which he devoured, often four or five at a time. His collection contained a number of first editions by authors as varied as James M. Cain, John .Fante, a Fitzgerald or two and, his favorite, Nick Tosches. He was currently immersed in recent biographies of his political heroes, Harry S. Truman and Winston Churchill.

Once, sitting around a table in a hotel bar with Johnny, the boss and a few others after a gig, he'd mentioned he'd been thinking of moving back home, the place where he was born. "Where's that, Pete?" Ms. Raitt inquired.

"Tuscaloosa, Alabama," he replied.

"Why on earth would you want to live down there with all those rednecks?" asked the befuddled redhead.

"Let me pull your coat, mama. My granddaddy owned a little grocery store and when the hurricane came and blew off his roof, who do you think helped him replace it? White men, those "rednecks" you refer to. As a little boy, I played with white *and* black kids. Sure, we couldn't go to school together, we couldn't drink from the same water fountain and I'd better not try to date your sister, but we all knew each other on a first name basis and hung out."

The table sat silent as he continued.

"We moved to New York, first Harlem, then up to White Plains. How many black people did most New Yorkers know back then? Their mailman and who else, maybe their kid's kindergarten teacher? The schools in New York weren't officially segregated like back home, but they zoned your ass out of the good ones, unless they needed a token Negro or two. Any honest black person will tell you, you scratch the surface of a New York liberal, and you'll find a raging bigot every time. I'd rather know where I stand than to be around those phonies grinning in my face."

No one knew what to say, but a look passed between Pete and Johnny, further cementing a bond that had lasted what seemed like a lifetime. For Johnny understood, having grown up New Orleans' French Quarter, where most Sicilians like himself lived within spitting distance of a Creole and black population. His father too, had owned a store, called Po-Boy's, which served the best Italian meatball and sausage sandwiches and *pasta e fagioli* in the city. The Quarter was the birthplace of the great Sicilian musicians, Louis Prima and his bandleader, Sam Butera.

Back in the present, both men returned to their rooms to pack their things. The girl looked up, as if to ask, what now?

"Well, first off, what's your name...and where you headed? Oh yeah, and are you of legal age?"

The girl took a breath and said, "My name is Paulette de Saint Marie. I live in Old Greenwich, Connecticut. And I really have no idea where I'm going. It said on the news that the electrical grid has been knocked out all over the entire northeastern sector of the country." She paused, gathering her thoughts and her courage, and then asked, "Can I go with you? I heard you on the phone and it sounded like you have family in New Orleans. Oh, and yes, I'm nineteen, perfectly legal."

Johnny asked, "You got a car, Boo?" She nodded. "And do you mind if we bring my friend?"

"There's plenty of room in my car. It's a brand new, white Beemer 700 series." She blushed, having caught herself boasting, and was immediately ashamed because she'd been raised better than that.

He smiled the smile that had charmed fifty years' worth of girls like her. "Go get washed up, baby; we goin' to New Orleans."

Depending on who's driving and the number of pit stops, the trip from Austin to New Orleans can take anywhere between seven and nine hours. The curious young girl wanted to stop and see sites like Lake Charles and Lafayette, the home of Tabasco Sauce, and a couple of historic plantations she'd googled, but Uncle Nicky kept calling every twenty minutes, urging Johnny to "Keep movin' baby. Fuckin' history is bein' made while you dawdle." So, with a heavy foot, and he and Pete switching off with Paulette, who was a faster driver than either man, they reached Metairie in seven hours and forty-five minutes, stopping only a few times for gas, a bag full of crawfish and to hit the bathroom.

Over the sound of Cajun music on the radio, as they passed through East Texas, Paulette related her family history. She was the great granddaughter of a French banking dynasty, the only true rivals of the more famous Rothschilds. So, she spoke fluent Parisian French but could barely make out the antiquated, 200-year old version of the language she was hearing spoken and sung on the radio.

Her father Jacques, a 33rd degree Freemason, traveled the world on family business, while her mother and two siblings lived in the lap of luxury in Old Greenwich. "That's *Old* Greenwich," she said laughingly, "as in Old Money. We live in a one hundred-year old, nineteen-room mansion on the Long Island Sound. I graduated last year from Greenwich Academy and was supposed to start at Yale this year but school bores the shit out of me, so I took off to travel and follow the music."

"Well, honey," said Johnny, "you gonna be around the best music in the world soon, so keep your ears open and you might learn something."

Encouraged by the guys' interest in what she had to say, she went on to describe the differences between Old Money and the *Nouveau Riche* who populated lower Westchester County and the show biz crowd out in Hollywood. "They like everything new and shiny, the latest stupid fashions. You know, the gold bathroom fixtures, big black SUVs or red Mercedes, all the latest gauche and gaudy fashion statements. Our style is subtler: worn carpets, frayed cuffs on shirts, a three-year old Buick station wagon in the driveway. The change in collar length from year to year is imperceptible. New Money needs to advertise itself; Old Money prefers anonymity. They feel they have nothing to prove."

Johnny got it, remembering how the real power back home always shielded itself from the public eye. Pete, too, was familiar with this phenom-enon from his extensive reading, not to mention his keen powers of obser-vation. They wound up liking this sharp kid, even before they reached their destination. She possessed the ease and comfort in the presence of all types of people that is the mark of true class.

The closer they got to the Crescent City, the funkier the music on the radio became. Johnny found a station at the right hand end of the dial that played New Orleans classics like Frogman Henry, Huey "Piano" Smith, Irma Thomas, Professor Longhair, Ernie K-Doe and of course, Fats Domino, who was singing "Walking To New Orleans," as they pulled off Interstate 10 into Jefferson Parish and on up to the guarded gate of Uncle Nicky Santoro's private compound in Metairie, home of the Louisiana Mafia.

CHAPTER 3

NICKY SANTORO, AT FIVE FEET, FOUR AND
one-half inches, stood taller than most men in his orbit. At ninety-eight
years of age, his grip was still powerful, as the much taller and physically
fit Pete Holman discovered, shaking off the pain of their handshake.

"That's some grip you got there, Mr. Santoro," said Pete. The older man's
eyes held Pete's, as he grinned the grin that had struck terror in many a
taller man over the past eighty-some years.

"It's Nicky. Call me Nicky. I like you son. You a friend of Johnny's, then
you okay with me. An' you, little girl. What's your name?"

"Paulette de Saint Marie, sir."

"You a Coon-ass, baby?"

Unfamiliar with the term, the question confused her. "What's a Coon-
ass? Do I look black?"

"No, *cher*, a Coon-ass is a Cajun," Nicky laughed heartily, "French, like
your name. That's what they call they selves. Most of 'em live on the bayous.
But you sound like you from the north, yeah?"

"Yes, Connecticut, Old Greenwich."

"Ah yeah, I know dat place. Then you daddy's rich, like me. What's
he do?"

"Well, yes, he's wealthy," she replied flatly, not bragging, just imparting
information. "He's in banking."

"This electric grid goin' down. That's gonna mess up his business, no? You talk to him yet? Where's he at now?"

"No sir, we haven't spoken. We've been driving for seven hours. He's in Paris on business."

"Well you got that phone there. You need to call him, girl. That's you daddy. You know he's worried about you. Don't be wastin' time."

Obediently, Paulette pressed the buttons of her father's number. Seven-thirty pm in New Orleans meant it was two-thirty am in Paris, but what with all the madness at home and unable to book a flight to New York, Jacques de Saint Marie was wide awake, and much relieved to hear his daughter's voice.

"Where are you, sweetheart? Are you all right? Have you spoken to Mother?"

"No, Daddy, I've been in the car all day and just now arrived in New Orleans. I'm with friends and I'm safe here at Mr. Santoro's house."

"I've been trying to call home. I suspect they will have electricity, as long as she has gasoline for the generator. But there appears to be no service, so I can't reach her phone. Who is Mr. Santoro?"

"Too complicated. He's my friend Johnny's uncle. He lives on a large compound."

"Who's Johnny? Is this Mr. Santoro with you now? May I speak with him, please?"

She handed the phone to Nicky, who went into full charm mode, to calm a worried father's fears. Pleasantries were exchanged and then he got down to business.

"Look-a here Jacques. Can I call you Jacques? You daughter perfectly safe here. We'll feed her and take good care of her, long as she needs, so you don't need to worry 'bout nothing."

"Thank you, Mr. Santoro. Anything she requires just let me know. Money is no object. Just, please, if you will, make sure she stays in touch."

"Money ain't no object on my end neither, brother. She tell me you a banker. So, I assume you a patriotic American. With all this mess goin' on over here, you an' me might can put our heads together and come up with a few things that can serve our country and make ourselves happy at the same time."

"I'm not sure exactly what you mean," said Jacques, cautiously. "Do you have something specific in mind?"

"Not just yet, but we'll be talkin', real soon. Now you take care and don't you worry 'bout nothing."

He handed the phone back to Paulette, satisfied that a piece of the puzzle had been put in place.

With the country in utter chaos and a sharply divided and partisan government unequipped to act cohesively in an emergency of this magnitude, Nicky had quickly and rightly perceived that the time was perfect to return *La Mafia* to its rightful place in America's pecking order. Certainly, the chaotic political climate was ripe for some kind of change.

In normal times, a crisis, even a much lesser one, would have galvanized the public, bringing opposing factions together as Americans, as had Pearl Harbor after December 7, 1941 or, to a lesser extent, 9/11, twenty years before.

But firebrands and anarchists on the far left had in recent years stirred up the gullible young, having convinced them that fascism was on the rise from the right, when anyone with eyes to see—like Nicky Santoro, for instance—could tell that the very opposite was true. The Republicans, for their part, were too incompetent and too fearful of their own shadows to accomplish anything worthwhile, much less their own goals, even if they could agree among themselves just what those goals were.

Tribalism and identity politics had separated and divided the public into dozens of groups, cliques of ignorant people too lazy to read past the headlines and who'd been led to believe they were all somebody's victim.

No doubt about it. The time was right.

At this point, Carmela Mancuso, Nicky's longtime housekeeper, who looked to be somewhere between eighty and ninety years of age, made her entrance.

Carmela was born and raised in St. Francisville in West Feliciana Parish, an upstate hamlet of a little more than one thousand inhabitants that locals claim is "one mile long and three feet wide." Orphaned by age 12, she somehow made her way to New Orleans, where she earned her daily bread by catering to the desires of pedophiles in the back alleys of the French Quarter. Nicky, not that much older himself, took pity on her and got her off the block and engaged her as his housekeeper. He taught her to read, and to count and stack in neat little piles the money brought in by the whores who worked for him. For this kindness, she remained loyal to him all these many years.

"You need somethin', Boss?"

"Yeah, get these nice people a coupla rooms ready, clean sheets, towels and all dat. Johnny and his girl in one room and his buddy Pete in another."

"You got it babe. I'm on it." She started to walk away, then turned and remembered, "Jimmy call and say he got a fresh buncha ersters, right off the boat. You want me to run over and get you some?"

"No, that's alright. Carmine in there makin' somethin' different. Go on now. Get to work."

Familiarity of this sort between employer and employee was not exactly unknown to Paulette, although the language of the servants in her family home was somewhat more deferential. The cheeky attitude shown by the elderly Ms. Mancuso toward this man whose fortune was very likely earned from no small amount of violence made her wonder if there was more to him than met the eye.

Carmela exited the room to perform her duties.

CHAPTER 4

PAULETTE'S MOTHER, PATRICIA DE SAINT MARIE, was born of Irish and German stock. Her maiden name was Ritter. She tended to drink a bit. Actually, more than a bit, a habit not uncommon among wives who had made The Bargain: their youth and beauty in exchange for the loneliness that can come with marriage to a man who can provide the creature comforts a woman with her attributes often sees as her due, but who has neither the time, nor energy, to be a husband in the emotionally nourishing sense.

Her family of origin was as middle class as they come. She had grown up in Norwalk, a couple towns up the coast from Jacques's family estate in Old Greenwich. Dreaming of rising up the socio-economic ladder, upon graduation from Norwalk's Central Catholic High School, she decided to forego college and instead use her looks and athletic ability at swimming, tennis and golf to get invited to the better country clubs in the area, where she could be seen by and meet the kind of man who might provide her with the life she coveted.

After dating one too many "jerk balls" who failed to see what she saw as the true value that lay beneath her surface beauty, she eventually met Jacques, who was smitten from the moment he saw her long, sun-tanned legs on the tennis court and determined to meet and possess this blonde goddess.

After a visit to his family home and upon meeting his parents, who were equally smitten with her, all that remained was to become pregnant in order to seal the deal. Greenwich's elite attended the wedding and only the most catty of the female friends of the groom's family noticed the slight bulge in the lovely bride's belly.

Eight months later, Paulette's brother Pierre, named after his great grandfather, founder of the French banking dynasty that bore the family name, was born and she followed ten months later. As in many such marriages, their subsequent sex life dwindled and, five years later, an unexpected sister, Michelle, was born, the product of a faulty diaphragm. For Patricia--Pat to her friends--two children had been more than enough to secure her future, and poor Michelle was a sadly unwelcome addition to her family.

And so, Pat began to drink during the day, first at the club and, in time, at home too. With Jacques traipsing back and forth across the Atlantic, handling the family business, her imbibing increased. With more than enough household help, nannies, maids, cooks and a chauffeur, the kids were well taken care of, lacking only what they needed most, parental love and affection. It affected Michelle the worst. By sixth grade, she was getting high and by her freshman year, had already done two stints in rehab.

Pierre was by now off to Yale in New Haven, leaving Paulette, as the middle child, the only sober family member at home full time. Her guidance counselor at Greenwich Academy recommended Al-Anon, for children of alcoholics and it did her some good, but she still felt isolated and spent much of her time alone in her room, with the music in which she sought solace. Brighter than her classmates, she graduated a year early and before long was attending shows and concerts, where the looks inherited from her mother got her invited backstage to meet these wondrous people who made the sounds that fed her soul.

Far less promiscuous by nature than most other backstage girls, she was selective in her choices of bedmates. In addition, she had an intense fear of STDs, so her night spent with Johnny Santoro was somewhat of an anomaly for her and, being a man of the world, he sensed her relative innocence and related to her accordingly.

Now, even in the wake of the failed electrical grid, Patricia de Saint Marie felt safe in her home. The help always kept a large stock of provisions in the pantry; so there would easily be a month's worth of food should the electricity fail to return soon. The large generator would power the mansion's elaborate security system, as well as the refrigerator and freezer, in case of looters. The chauffeur was armed with an old Colt 45 revolver and, after the first sign of trouble in the next town, the system alerted two armed guards to come and stand in position outside the entrances.

What Patricia did not know was, that in the nearby city of Stamford, rioting had already begun. There was looting, as frightened citizens scrambled to gather as much food and water as they could find. But soon, roving packs of these looters were breaking into stores, running out with giant, now useless TVs, computers, cameras or jewelry, anything they thought they could sell or exchange for food and water. Liquor stores were, as always, the first to be hit. Gang bangers smashed pharmacy windows, stealing everything that even looked like a drug. Hysterical hoards of obese women were robbing clothing and lingerie they'd never be able to squeeze their fat, bloated bodies into.

And then, the shooting began. Snipers on rooftops, one gang settling old scores with another, angry blacks shooting at cops, fearful whites ready to pull the trigger on anyone who even looked like they didn't belong in their neighborhood.

From Old Greenwich, one could now see the smoke rising a few miles away in Stamford. Bridgeport, a rough town to begin with, took no time turning into a version of Beirut. For the time being, Greenwich appeared to be safe. But the local police force, which in normal times had only to worry about drunken college kids during school holidays and the occasional thieves from the poorer towns like Port Chester, just across the border in New York breaking into homes, was inadequate to handle the kind of trouble that might, and as it turned out, was bound to occur.

It wouldn't be long before cell phone batteries wore down and, with no way to recharge, communication soon became impossible. Gas pumps, run by electricity, could pump no gas. The only saving grace was that it was still early September; so heating would not be needed.

The bigger cities, with their large populations of the poor, were the first to turn into war zones, as panic rose when people began to encounter empty shelves in food stores. Stupidly, some stole meat, which, without working refrigeration, would go bad within twenty-four hours. The same would be true for frozen items. One solution was to cook up any meat and frozen food right away and share with neighbors and friends while it was still edible. The only safe thing to eat was that old standby, canned food. Spam was among the first items to go. Vegetarians and vegans began to panic, as items on their menus were even harder to come by under these circumstances.

Pete Holman knew this was how things would go in Greenburgh, where blacks and Italians had lived in a kind of harmony for as many as four generations in that unchanging part of town. If the lack of electricity shut down the gas so the stoves wouldn't work, he knew the folks there would barbeque. Others would go up to the dam and catch fish to eat. But how long could this last? Still, he wished he were there to care for his mom and sister.

Caring for his family was never again going to be something Johnny would have to contend with. There was still no news about which of America's many enemies the bomb had come from, nor even whether it had been from a missile or a dirty bomb smuggled into the country, or one of the home-grown anti-government leftist or right-wing activist groups that had been multiplying over the past decade.

As evening turned into night, and his fight-or-flight adrenaline wore off, images of his loved ones lost in LA filled his heart, and he thought of those he would never see or hold in his arms again. He'd been able to block those feelings all day, knowing he needed to be strong for the others and get them to the safety of his uncle's compound. But now, sitting alone on the bed, he could no longer hold back the emotions and he began to weep. An overwhelming sense of loss now came hard and fast, as he sobbed into a pillow, hoping no one might hear.

He had borne a similar loss during the first years after his divorce, but in the back of his mind there'd always been the hope that things might one day be repaired, enough at least that the barely civil might advance to a kind of tepid affection if nothing more. His second ex-wife, Robin, was the daughter of a television director and worked as a talent agent specializing in the area of TV commercials, securing work for actors and actresses who, while they might lack the charisma or sex appeal necessary for stardom, could still work at their craft under the illusion that their big break was just around the next corner.

These delusional souls arrived in Hollywood by the hundreds each day, most winding up as waiters, Uber drivers, yoga instructors or other menial jobs that allowed them the freedom to go on the endless rounds of auditions that led nowhere except perhaps to the bed of someone like her father, a seducer and womanizer of the lowest order, which went a long way toward understanding why a bright woman like Robin might consider a touring guitar player potential husband material.

As a musician, although not a soloist, Johnny was one of the finest rhythm guitarists around, also one of the better band conductors, one who commanded the respect of other players, which explained why he was seldom out of work. When that did occur, though, it was Robin who supported him and their two children, helping to keep up the mortgage on the modest house in Studio City, on Landale Street, called "musicians' row," because so many others in his profession lived there.

As a husband, he was, shall we say, lacking. And what he lacked most of all was the wherewithal to resist the temptations of the road, namely those women who throw themselves at men who earn their living playing music onstage. An egoless sideman who had no desire for fame, he understood that his job was to make the boss look good. In that capacity, he excelled. He had the ability to anticipate the singer's fluffs and make them look intentional. He knew when to raise the volume or change the tempo at the end of a bridge section to create an emotional peak for the audience, often causing them to applaud in the middle of a song. The singer, thinking this was her own doing, nevertheless paid him handsomely for this skill.

Johnny purposely accepted the background role, yet women sought him out after the show. He had an uncanny ability to avoid the more troublesome ones, those with social diseases or psychotic tendencies. He was also careful not to fool around in town. Almost always. There was that one time when his motto of "Don't shit where you eat" failed to keep his libido or his heart in check.

Her name was Brittney. Twenty-five years old, with long, dark brown hair that hung to the middle of her back and more beautiful than any movie star, she inexplicably had no desire to be either an actress or a model. That was what first attracted him. A receptionist at the agency where his wife worked, she never failed to get up from her desk and greet him with a hug and that brilliant smile whenever he came by the office. In time, her hugs turned to kisses, at first on his cheek and later on his lips. Her specialty was to place her hands on either side of his face as she kissed him with her beautiful green eyes open wide. By then, he was hooked. The occasional lunch turned into a full-blown affair. She'd call his house from work, leaving flirtatious messages, hinting of what might be, until one day Robin heard her voice on his answering machine and picked up. "You little whore, this ends now. Stay away from my husband or I'll break those pretty little teeth of yours."

The affair continued, the secrecy making it all the more exciting. Brittney got off on the competition with the older woman. Robin eventually had enough and ended the marriage. Her annual income was slightly more than Johnny's so, under California law, there was no alimony. The children were by then grown and living on their own, so child support was not an issue either. As divorce settlements go, this one was not so difficult, despite the bitterness of losing one's husband to a much younger woman.

His adult daughter, Stacy, had had problems for some time, even prior to her parents' split. Partying, drinking, drugs, poor choices in men, herpes, the usual LA panoply of issues. She'd run off at 18 to Palm Springs for a wild weekend with some girlfriends. She woke up the next morning with a bad headache, lying between a bartender from the hotel and some other guy she didn't even remember meeting the night before.

The other girls went home Sunday night and by Monday morning she'd hooked up with the bartender and was staying at his place. He got her a job at the restaurant as a hostess because, he said, she was "too hot to be nothing but a waitress." The money wasn't enough to keep them in cocaine, so he made a connection and started dealing weed to certain trusted customers. When that still wasn't enough, he began introducing her to special guests of the hotel, and conned her into turning the occasional trick, "just for now, baby, until we get on our feet."

Once every week or two turned into two or three times a week and, before she knew it, she was bringing in as much as a thousand a night. One of these clients turned out to be a local cop, who demanded a cut in return for "fixing" any future beefs.

A friend of Johnny's who sang old standards and played piano in the hotel bar, phoned him on the road to let him know what was up with Stacy and Johnny went to his uncle for help. Nicky called a friend in Palm Springs and one night after work the two of them were grabbed by three big guys as they were about to get in their car.

Stacy managed to let out one scream before a strip of gaffer's tape across her lips silenced her. They were taken in an SUV out to the desert where she was forced to watch as the boyfriend was beaten to within an inch of his life and dumped into a ditch with a warning to never come near Stacy again. She was then driven back to her mother's house on Landale Street and told to "be a good girl and don't get into any more trouble."

Seeing her lover boy left lying in the desert sand next to a cactus with his pants down around his ankles and two broken kneecaps should've shown her the light, but instead she was furious and called Johnny the next morning. It was one of those "Daddy, how could you?" monologs after which she slammed the phone down, before he had a chance to speak. But, at least she was safe. She cursed and yelled to her mother.

"Mom, Daddy called his Mafia friends on us! They almost killed my boyfriend! He's a fucking monster!"

Robin listened silently to her daughter's hysterics, letting the girl vent, until she wore herself out and sat there with her face in her hands at the kitchen table, crying. Her little brother came in and put his head in her lap, wrapping his arms around her waist.

"I'm so fucking stupid Mom. Why do I do this shit?"

It was that moment of clarity, the opening Robin had been waiting and hoping for.

"It's going to be alright, sweetie. We'll get through this, okay? How about I fix you a nice, hot bath, huh?"

With no place to go, no job and no money, Stacy was stuck at home with her mom and brother. The return to a normal family life gave her some stability and she eventually got sober and, after a couple years, was on the verge of rapprochement with her father when the bomb struck.

Coming out of the shower, Paulette now stood at the door to the room of the man she'd met less than twenty-four hours earlier. Not wishing to intrude or make him self-conscious, she waited, until that inner child of an alcoholic told her to go to him. Tip-toeing over, she put her arms around him, softly at first, then more tightly as if to contain his sobs. She pressed her face against his back, hoping to impart her own strength and empathy to him through osmosis.

His sobbing eventually subsided. He turned to her and they lay together, wordlessly, in each other's arms. With her thumbs, she wiped away his tears and she kissed his eyelids. Once she was sure he was calmed, she got up and removed his shoes and clothing and then her own and got them both under the covers.

The world had changed, perhaps forever. There would be time in the morning to learn more about what was going on, in the country, and in the world as a result of this horrible act of barbarity. But for now, sleep came as a blessing, deep enough for there to be no ugly dreams. Only peace.

CHAPTER 5

WITH THE NORTHEASTERN SECTOR OF THE nation incommunicado, there were still many square miles-worth of citizens between there and the West Coast who needed the comforting words of their president, or whomever was in charge. An unprecedented occurrence like this would've tested the mettle of even an experienced administration, but to expect anything even resembling sober leadership from a wise-cracking professional comedian and her cabinet of show biz cronies would have been cruelly unfair.

The unelected bureaucrats who typically run the government, year after year and administration after administration, were pretty much as worthless as the computers sitting lifelessly on their desks in Washington and everywhere else that lacked electricity. Thus, it was left to the military to take charge, quietly and behind the scenes, so as not to further panic the public.

President Silverman was placed aboard Air Force One, along with several members of the Joint Chiefs of Staff, speechwriters, Secret Service personnel, hair and make-up artists and other handlers, including her wardrobe person and a couple of now-superfluous gag writers, all headed toward an undisclosed location in an underground bunker under a mountain somewhere in the wilds of Wyoming. For a presidential speech needed to be written and delivered in short order to comfort the masses.

During the flight, cooler heads strove to impress upon the naïve head of state the importance of appearing serious and in control of the situation. At first, she balked, trying to explain that what she'd promised her voters was "a new kind of presidency, one where The People would always know what their president was feeling at any moment of the day or night."

Eyes rolled at this drivel and two of the highest-ranking generals plus one admiral attempted to put things into perspective for the person they'd taken an oath to serve. Seeing Silverman was prepared to throw her constitutional weight around, General Colleen McQuarter, who was the Marine Commandant, took her aside and spoke to her privately, woman to woman.

"Ma'am, you are the Commander-in-Chief of the greatest nation the world has ever known and, with all due respect to the office to which the citizens of this country elected you, we both know that you do not have the first inkling of what the fuck you are doing. You know as well as I do that you were only elected as a big 'Fuck you' to what came before, and for no other earthly reason."

"But, but…"

"No buts. The nation is in dire straits. No one knows what or who may be coming for us next. The country must have confidence that *someone* is in control. You or whoever speaks to them in your stead must exude total confidence that all will be well…and soon."

The president nodded, as the gravity of the situation in which she found herself finally began to dawn on her.

"Now, here is what is going to happen. You are going to put on your big girl pants and go on the air and deliver a speech, word-for-word, as written, and with all the seriousness and dignity of the office you hold. No adlibs. No jokes. Or else…" pausing for effect, she continued, "with great sadness, the country will be told that unknown assailants somehow managed to assassinate you and the vice president and, therefore, for the time being until the Speaker of the House can be located, the military shall be in charge."

"You're going to 'disappear' me, aren't you? You're going to fucking kill me!" Sarah Silverman did not rise in the treacherous ranks of Hollywood by being stupid.

"You have a choice, Ms. President. For the good of your country, which will it be? We land in thirty-five minutes. I'll need your answer by then. I hope you make the right decision."

CHAPTER 6

AS IT SO HAPPENED, THE CURRENT LEADER OF THE
Senate was one Antonino "Handsome Tony" Calabrese of Louisiana, and
a close friend of Nicola "Nicky" Santoro of Metairie.

As was his lifelong habit, Nicky Santoro was wide awake at four-thirty
am, checking the news, the European stock market and generally gathering any and all information needed to stay on top of his rivals around the
country and across the globe. By five, sipping a *cornetto*, and nibbling the
cookie-like rusk hard bread called *fette biscottate* or the bread roll known
as a *tramezzino*, he was ready to receive the *omaggio*, or tribute, from
his *capos'* endeavors of the previous evening, the revenue derived from
gambling, prostitution, and other netherworld activities, including the
sale of narcotics.

At seven am, Johnny and Paulette, as well as Pete in the next room,
were awakened by the sound of Jessie Hill singing "Ooh Poo Pah Doo" on
a radio somewhere, as well as the aroma of bacon, scrambled eggs, fried
potatoes, peppers, onions, Italian sausage and freshly-baked Italian bread.

There were few things Johnny loved more at breakfast time than a
sandwich made from these ingredients. Offering Paulette a bite of the hot
salsiccia, the girl's eyes began to water and perspiration formed on the
crown of her head, but gamely she swallowed the spicy meat, hoping to
show she was one of the guys.

After breakfast, Nicky showed her to the stables, where she was introduced to Antoine Dumaine, a tiny Creole former jockey, not much bigger than Nicky, who cared for the horses. The night before, Paulette had mentioned that she rode in equestrian competitions at home and had, in fact, won some prizes, being fairly expert in the various disciplines, including dressage, reining, obstacles and show jumping. She loved horses and they always responded to her loving nature.

"Pick her out a nice one 'Twan and take her out on the trails, as long as she wants." Nicky sent along one of his guys, as a bodyguard, remembering his promise to her father.

Antoine chose a beautiful golden Palomino and asked if she preferred to ride English or Western. "Will he let me ride bareback?" she asked and Antoine smiled, realizing that, with a real horsewoman to guide around the enormous property, the morning would not be a boring one. She quickly made friends with the steed and he responded in kind, recognizing a horse lover when he met one.

The three mounted and headed off and Antoine called out to her, "He knows all the trails. You could fall asleep on him and he'll get you back home. And you can ride as fast as you like, so don't worry; we'll keep up with you," and at that, Paulette took off at a medium gallop, the groom and the bodyguard not far behind. The two Golden Retrievers that trailed after them gave up after a half mile and trotted back to the stables.

It was exhilarating, the wind blowing, causing her ponytail to snap against her bare neck and shoulders as her long legs held tightly to the Palomino's saddleless torso. As they learned each other's moves, horse and rider soon became one, he, thankful to be led by one who knew what she was doing and she, thrilled by the exquisite beauty and responsiveness of the powerful beast. Antoine, riding English as in his jockey days, had no problem keeping up, unlike the hefty guard, who struggled and bounced along behind on a bulky Western saddle.

The air was thick with Louisiana humidity, exaggerated by proximity to the lake, so the damp wind felt twice as good on her skin. She observed the subtropical flower and fauna as she rode through the marshy wetlands. She wondered at all the rabbits, squirrels, tree frogs, a snake or two, a turtle, a fox scurrying off and even a deer standing so still as to be practically unnoticeable. In the air, there were several pelicans and Dumaine pointed out a great white egret as it took off, its giant wingspan giving it its magnificent power of flight. They stopped and dismounted when he pointed out a red-cockaded woodpecker, one of several rare endangered species indigenous to the state of Louisiana. He identified it for her by the small patch of scarlet on the side of its head. The small bird pecked away, to Paulette's delight, finding its breakfast of insects in the rotting wood of a dead bald cypress tree.

During the hours she rode, back at the house, a constant flow of information was being gathered, deciphered and brought to Nicky in his office, where he further pulled it apart and put it back together like a great puzzle, finding ways in which he could weaponize it for purposes known only to himself. For his ancient mind was always six moves ahead of anyone else's.

"Get hold of that old Coon-ass Landry and get his ass down here. I need him," he ordered an assistant, "An' tell them chirren I want 'em here after lunch too."

George Landry was the king of the Cajuns and was in charge of the bayou towns around Lafayette and north to Alexandria and Monroe. Operating out of the small town of Rayne, known as the "Frog Capitol of the World," he'd reported and paid tribute to Nicky Santoro in the years since the passing of Carlos Marcello.

The "chirren" were Nicky's brilliant concession to modernity, a group of young millennial computer nerds, all expert hackers, equal to any in the world, that he had monetized and kept on generous salaries to serve his nefarious purposes. As an extra, sobering incentive, it was made known to each that the welfare and safety of their families depended on their loyalty to him and only him.

One of his few legitimate, and profitable, businesses had come courtesy of these kids. He'd mentioned his need for a means of conducting long distance conversations with associates without the likelihood of eavesdropping by nosey federal agents. What the kids came up with was a Skype-like app Nicky named Skootch, after his late brother, Johnny's father, who'd overseen bookie operations throughout the city of New Orleans. He set up a small corporation to sell this app to a select few for big bucks. It was also extremely valuable in his personal dealings.

Since the moment Los Angeles was destroyed the previous morning and the northeastern power grid was shut down, the kids had been scouring the web at Nicky's behest for the source of the problem, trying to find a way to fix it and, hopefully, to identify who was behind both events. They'd been told to ignore LA for the time being; there'd be time for that later. Anyway, it was the government's problem, not his. Orders were--not to fix the grid—but just to find a way how and then report to Nicky once they had it. He expected a solution by after lunch.

Even amidst the chaos resulting from the power outage, there was always the possibility that the phone lines were being tapped, including cell phones. Once the kids taught Nicky how to use this Skootch, his private conversations remained hidden from curious government eyes and ears. Still, the next steps in his plans were too important to take any chances, hence the post-lunch, in-person meeting with his kids was held in his lead-lined, windowless room built especially for such special purposes.

Lunch was prepared in the large kitchen, the dimensions of a medium-sized restaurant and equipped with the finest stove, oven, stainless steel refrigerator, freezer, pots, pans and utensils available. The chef was a third-generation *Napoletan*, whose father and grandfather had worked for Carlos Marcello and, since the older man's passing, for Nicky.

Carmine was well versed in the preparation of any number and kinds of cuisines, from the finest gourmet treats from around the world to the peasant dishes of virtually every nation on the globe, his specialties being Nicky's favorite Southern Italian and the Creole cooking of his hometown.

Today's luncheon consisted of lobster bisque and shrimp gumbo with Italian sausage, both of which made Johnny and Pete's mouths water and, although these dishes were foreign to Paulette, were a treat to her taste buds, as well. Brought up with genteel manners, she made sure to compliment the chef and shake his hand, addressing him by his Christian name.

For dessert, there were Pecan praline bars and beignets, along with Creole bread pudding with Bourbon sauce. In Pete's honor, there was the peach cobbler he'd mentioned in passing. Paulette was stuffed but couldn't resist a nibble of praline. Pete had the cobbler, while Johnny was crazy about the beignets and ate three, which rendered him ready for a nap afterwards.

But there was no time for napping, as Nicky's "chirren" were due to show up soon and he wanted Johnny at the meeting. Landry arrived on time, as was his habit. His presence was desired because, despite his family background of professional alligator hunters, he was up on the modern world of the Internet, sufficiently to be able to speak the jargon and comprehend much, if not most, of what was said.

The nerds' report was good, in that it made the boss happy, or it began that way. They told him they'd hacked their way into the electrical grid. At first, it led them to the Russians, and then they were misdirected to Iran, but both of these turned out to be false leads, made to appear that way by some third party hoping perhaps to incite the Americans to an unwarranted war. The trail bounced around the world and back again to the United States. They had nothing definite yet, but it was looking as though the source might be in Minnesota, giving the kids the impression that it may have been the work of some Islamic terrorist group, perhaps ISIS or Hamas sleeper cells or even a lone wolf radicalized by watching terrorist YouTube videos. Cities and towns, all over the state, contained huge, growing Middle Eastern populations in recent decades, so this conclusion wasn't all that unlikely.

"Don't fucking give me no 'Perhaps,' I pay you to *know*, not no god damn guesswork," said Nicky, without raising his voice, which was never a good sign. When a man is about to unleash the kind of power a Nicky Santoro had at his disposal, there is no room for assumption or speculation.

"Go back to work, and don't come back here till you positive. Got it?"

When they'd gone, Landry spoke first. "What we gonna do, Nicky? We can't make no move unless we know exactly who we up against. I got my boys from upstate and East Texas chompin' at the bit, ready to go, man. We need these *gamins* to get busy, *Patron*, yeah?"

"Yeah, you got that right."

While Johnny was meeting with his uncle and George Landry, Paulette returned to the bedroom to check her phone for messages and lie down and rest her eyes for a few moments. In the hallway, she ran into Carmela Mancuso. Never one to hold her tongue, Carmela always came right out with what was on her mind.

"You a little young for Johnny, ain't you, Boo? You a cute little piece though, nice an' polite too. I jus' hope you ain't thinkin' of takin' no advantage. We love that boy. I known him since before he could pee straight. Changed his little pissy diapers many a time. An' I seen his little dicky bird probly more times than you," she grinned.

TMI, Paulette was thinking, *too much information*. And yet she found herself liking this old crone in spite of it. In fact, she liked everybody she'd met in Johnny's circle so far. She'd never met characters like these before but somehow felt completely at ease with them.

She thought about how, or even whether, to answer Carmela's concerns without seeming to brag about her own circumstances, so she simply replied, "No worries Carmela, I really do like him. A lot."

"I thought so. You got that look in them pretty eyes. Just be nice to him, hon. He a good man. Got a tender heart, that boy. Don't hurt him."

She gave Paulette's cheek a little pinch, and went on about her business.

CHAPTER 7

BY LATE AFTERNOON IN THE NORTHEAST SECTOR,
cell phone batteries were running low and the only means police had of
remaining in communication were by way of their car radios. There was
plenty of gasoline in the underground tanks at police stations but, without
electricity, there was no easy way to pump it. To ration fuel, driving was
kept at a minimum. Arrangements were being made to syphon, but that
would be time consuming in an emergency. Younger officers and civilian
volunteers were put in charge of this solution.

Looting, rioting, arson and random shooting were all continuing
in Stamford and in every city, large and small, throughout the area. In
Manhattan, Boston, Philadelphia, Baltimore, Cleveland, Chicago and
other cities, office workers were forced to take the stairs down from the
upper reaches of tall buildings, as elevators were not working. More than
a few of these had heart attacks or strokes and had to be carried down by
younger and stronger people.

The lives of Old Greenwich residents who'd had the foresight to
purchase generators and a supply of gasoline, were not much changed. The
ugly and fashionable solar panels had not been popular among residents
who preferred their homes to retain the old, traditional look. Guards from
the Di Paulo Security firm were working overtime to keep their clients safe
from predators. Patricia de Saint Marie, with a healthy supply of gin and

vermouth, was feeling no pain, and her younger daughter Michelle was emotionally immune, so long as her supply of cannabis held out.

Pat hadn't heard from either of her older two children and worried for their safety, but Jacques had finally managed to get through with words of support, but only until the battery in her cell phone died. By the time she recharged it in the guards' car, she could no longer get through to her husband in Paris.

There, an ocean away, life went on, pretty much as usual. Typically, Parisians cared little about the Americans' problems, as long as they could count on them for protection from enemies, potential and otherwise. This current situation in the United States was cause for some consternation, not only for France but for other Western European allies as well. Who knew what advantage might be taken from the East now, especially with a dubious, inexperienced American celebrity president who had yet to surface since this thing began?

And then there was China who, many feared, had been waiting to pounce for some time, ever since several previous administrations had chosen to ignore the Chinese buildup of their navy, until it greatly outnumbered America's outmoded fleet. China was high on the list of suspects for the electrical grid problem, since they had mounted numerous cyber attacks on U.S. corporations in recent years.

As a powerful and respected member of the second largest banking family in Europe, Jacques met with the French prime minister and his cabinet, along with France's most prominent business leaders as an ad hoc ambassador, in an effort to calm the waters until word from the States came through.

During a break in the meetings, he took a call from the area code 504. It was his daughter.

"Daddy, have you spoken with Mother yet?"

"Yes dear, but only briefly until her phone died out. How are things where you are?"

"I'm actually enjoying it here. I went riding this morning, on the most beautiful horse. Listen, do you have time to talk to Mr. Santoro?"

"Of course, darling, please put him on."

"Hey there Jacques, Nicky here. Your girl's havin' the time of her life. She lovin' our food. We gonna fatten her up real good for you."

He paused, thinking of the right approach to the delicate subject he wished to discuss, and to feel out Jacques regarding whether he might be a willing ally in what he had planned.

The sound of Jacques' voice broke into these thoughts, "Mr. Santoro, ah Nicky, I cannot sufficiently express my gratitude to you for keeping my little girl safe during this time of strife in our land. If ever I can do anything for you, you need only to ask."

"Now that you mention it, things on this side of the water ain't goin' real good. Can I be honest with you? I got friends in Congress tellin' me things in Washington need to change. This country been good to me an' you. I was thinkin' we might could put our heads together an' do somethin' to help out. You know, give somethin' back."

"I agree Nicky, we owe it to our nation to give back in any way we are able. Have you anything specific in mind?"

"Well, you know France and America always been friends. My people and me are not exactly unknown over there where you are. We especially strong in Marseille, see, but I could use a little help on your end of things. We dealt with them Rothschilds in the past, but I don't trust them and I got a good feelin' about you. I got some ideas about how to fix things over here, but it's gonna take money. Don't get me wrong, I got plenty money, but it's gonna take a whole bunch more."

"I see," pausing to consider Nicky's possible motives, and then, "Marseille, you say?"

"Yeah, and other spots too. I got friends all over. I'm a friendly guy. Friends is important, don't you think, Jacques? I'd like to think we friends, yeah?"

Marseille was a hint Nicky had tossed out, as a throwaway to see if Jacques would take the bait but Jacques hesitated, pondering its deeper meaning, but then remembering his daughter was in this man's hands. Then, playing for time,

"Absolutely, Nicky. Listen, I'm rushing out to another meeting but, by all means, let's continue this discussion. It won't be easy until everything gets straightened out, but we should definitely keep the conversation going."

They said their goodbyes and disconnected, and Nicky felt progress was being made, however slowly. The hook had been dangled and the worm was wiggling. He smiled to himself.

CHAPTER 8

BY NIGHTFALL, STAMFORD WAS IN SHAMBLES.
Downtown, not one storefront window remained unbroken. Merchandise, busted and smashed, was strewn all over the sidewalks and overflowing into the streets. Cars, left abandoned where they'd run out of fuel, were on fire or turned over, stripped of anything of value. In supermarkets, not one morsel of food remained on the shelves. Stores, whose owners had taken the precaution of posting signs saying "Black owned," were not spared. Intermittent gunshots could be heard sporadically.

Packs of as many as ten to twenty adolescents, many heavily armed, roamed the streets, filled with a dangerous mixture of unfocused rage and unacknowledged fear, causing terror among the otherwise law-abiding citizenry. Working class adults, long grown used to an overprotective government, and now left to their own devices, devolved into mob rule in a *milieu* reminiscent of *Lord of the Flies*.

In their search for escape from, and to take advantage of, the chaos, predatory mobs spread out to the better neighborhoods and towns, first Darien, then Greenwich and Cos Cob, and finally the peninsula of Old Greenwich, some eventually finding their way to the cul-de-sac on the Long Island Sound that ended at the home of Patricia de Saint Marie.

One of the two guards from Di Paulo Security had been called away to assist in a local police emergency, leaving only the older man, plus the family chauffeur and his ancient firearm for protection.

At approximately 8 pm, a dozen or so gangbangers from either Stamford or Port Chester, descended upon the dead-end street. One of them, the likely leader, recognized the de Saint Marie home from a party he'd once crashed there. Michelle, at the height of her druggie days, occasionally opened the house to her dope fiend friends when her parents were out of town and she had the place to herself. This gangbanger had dealt drugs to her once or twice.

Seeing the approaching crew, the remaining guard, realizing the car was gone and he had no way of calling for reinforcements, drew his gun, and said, "Hold it right there. This is private property."

"What'choo gonna do, old man? Get outa the fuckin' way."

He laughed and one of his boys fired, missing the guard. The chauffeur came out and, his hand shaking, pointed his pistol. Another banger shot, the bullet passing through his carotid artery. The guard returned fire and in a hail of bullets was hit three times, fatally. Inside, the female help screamed and ran this way and that, two to the kitchen, another upstairs to the maids' quarters on the third floor and still another locking herself in a basement lavatory.

Hearing the commotion and in a martini haze, Patricia peeked out the window and, seeing the guard and chauffeur lying on the ground surrounded by these young men with guns in their hands, stood frozen and nervously bit her manicured thumb.

The thugs entered the house, knocking over furniture at random, shooting wildly at the walls and ceiling.

"Let's go up and see if that little bitch got any drugs on her," said the leader as he and several others ascended the stairs and stormed one room after another, winding up in the master bedroom where Patricia stood, too frightened to scream. For who was there to hear?

The leader, named Tupac Prentiss, after his mother's favorite hip hop performer, went by the street name of Lil T, due to his small stature. Like many of his height, Tupac suffered from a Napoleon complex. He wore baggy garments, in an attempt to disguise his size. He wore his hair in corn rows and there was a gang tattoo visible on the left side of his neck.

He strutted over to her and grabbed her hair, pulling her backward, and thrust his other hand between her legs as the others watched, becoming aroused at the little man's brazen exhibition of power.

"Who want some a' this?" he shouted loudly, as he held her upright by her blonde hair, "After me, of course." He tore open her blouse and squeezed her breast. She screamed, "No, please," and he struck her in the face, knocking her to the bed, then, lifting her tennis skirt, lowered his loose pants and took her as she tried to fight him off, digging her fingernails into his face, cursing him until his hand, squeezing tightly around her throat, caused her to pass out.

When he'd done with her, the rest pounced, one after another according to the group's pecking order, in an ugly scene of rage, power and brutality that left her sobbing and bleeding on the king size bed that had been the place where she'd made love to her husband in happier times. In that moment, she knew she would never again be able to sleep there soundly, much less ever again feel sexual desire on that mattress.

Down the hall, behind her closed door, Michelle sat cross-legged, impervious on her bed, stoned and listening to music through her earphones, unable to hear either the shooting or her mother's screams. As Patricia was being violated, the girl's former nannie, Janie, the household's oldest servant, slipped up the back stairs and pulled her away, down the hall and out the rear door, across the lawn to the room above the garage where she and her husband, the chauffeur lived.

There, they were safe for the time being. She held Michelle in her arms, as she had when she was an infant and said, "Be still, honey, we'll be alright here. Terrible things are going on in the house. Just keep quiet. I got you."

The bangers tore through the house, grabbing anything they recognized as of value, too stupid to think about food and water, and trashing anything they didn't think they could sell, including the priceless art Jacques had brought back from Europe.

Then, as suddenly as they came, they left, to rape, pillage and vandalize elsewhere.

Sitting in the dark above the garage, Janie and Michelle heard them leave, shooting their guns into the air and shouting their triumph over those weaker than themselves, waving the open bottles of expensive liquor in their hands, as if it were the cheap wine they normally drank.

Janie and Michelle made their way to Pat's room, to find her in a pool of her own blood, from the blows to her face and her torn vagina and rectum. She lay there in a state of shock.

"Run to the bathroom and get me some hot towels, baby," whispered Janie, and the child obeyed.

"Oh mom," she cried softly as she left, looking plaintively toward the nannie. "Is she going to be okay?"

"Don't worry, honey, I got this. Go!" and the old woman began the task of administering to her employer, knowing that any hopes of finding a doctor in the middle of this crisis were out of the question. "Now, go find me some peroxide and alcohol…and anything you got for pain. She's gonna need it, once the shock wears off."

Sometime after midnight, the bedroom land line rang. It was Jacques, a little after 6 am in Paris. Janie picked up and told him as much of what had happened as she thought he could stand to hear. He broke down in tears and said there were still no planes leaving for the States and asked to speak to his wife.

"She's asleep, Mr. Jacques. I don't think we should wake her. She's been through more than any woman should have to bear."

He asked for Michelle and, before handing her the phone, Janie warned her to stay as calm as possible, so as not to panic her father. Their conversation was brief, each trying to console and not upset the other, since Jacques was helpless on the other end.

"Darling, please tell your mother I'll be home as soon as humanly possible. I love you, sweetheart. You must be strong for her."

Michelle was aching to get high but knew she couldn't. Even if she'd wanted to, the bangers had found her stash before they left, and taken every seed and every pill they could find, other than a few Percocet she had hidden away for emergencies. These she handed over to Janie for when her mother would need them.

CHAPTER 9

BY MORNING, NICKY SANTORO'S YOUNG NERDS
had found the source of the power outage, but not yet who the perpetrators
might be. They had reached the point in their work where they were able to
revive the grid, but, per Nicky's instructions, held off, awaiting his wishes.

"Good work, chirren. Don't make a move till I give you the word." He
then pressed another line on his old 1960s style office telephone and dialed
his friend, Senator Antonino Calabrese at his home, in the upscale neighborhood known as Lakeshore/Lake Vista, one of the few undamaged by
Hurricane Katrina in 2005. Bordered on the north by Lake Pontchartrain,
it had been built on reclaimed land and was protected by a seawall that had
been constructed in the 1920s.

Tony liked the fact that his refurbished 1939 home stood on a "super-
block," devoid of thru-streets with non-intersecting vehicular and pedestrian networks, rendering it relatively safe from criminals and other
undesirable elements. His house was surrounded by a thick, six-foot wall
and its entrance faced a walk-through lane, rather than the street. Every
Sunday morning, when not in Washington, D.C., he attended seven o'clock
mass at St. Pius X Roman Catholic Church on Spanish Fort Boulevard,
seated prominently with his wife and children in the first row of pews
immediately to the right-hand side of the center aisle, providing him both
prominence and easy egress.

Tony picked up on the first ring and, recognizing his friend's private number on the screen, said, "Hey, Nicky, what's shakin'? Where 'yat? Got good news for me?"

As was their habit, the men spoke in their New Orleans patois as a form of code meant to confuse the curious.

"It's ready, jus' waitin' to press the button, boy. What's shakin' on your end?"

"Seems our president has left the building, son. According to my good friends at the alphabet, she done gone to the angels, to dat Oval Office in the sky. And the *faux* dago with her. Did you know that mother fucker's real name was Warren Wilhelm, Junior? What's he, a fuckin' Nazi with a name like that?"

By all this unintelligible, apparent jabber was meant that the comedian cum president known as Sarah Silverman was no longer among the living, which Calabrese had heard from his contacts at the FBI and CIA. Vice President de Blasio, he of the bogus Italian surname, was also deceased.

"Aw, ain't that a shame. An' just when we thought we had our first guinea vice prez, huh?" The two Sicilians shared a laugh. "So, what's next?"

"Well, the Speaker of the House can't be found neither, so looks like the military's gonna have to take charge, for now, at least. Name's Marine General Colleen McQuarter. Not one of ours, a Mick I think, but I hear she might could be dealt with."

"You know the old joke: What do you call a dead politician? A good start. No offense." The old friends laughed again. "Throw the switch?" Nicky's code for turning the grid back on.

"No time like the present, I'd say."

"Catch you 'while ago baby," Nicky said, and proceeded to text his nerds the agreed upon code to give them the go ahead.

An hour and a half later, the kids had the grid up and running. All the best and brightest cyber experts in government service had no idea what had changed or why, but all across the Northeastern sector, computers,

TVs and appliances that had been left plugged in when the electricity went out were exploding with the sudden surge of power. It would be some time before these items could be replaced and things were back to some semblance of normalcy.

CHAPTER 10

AT NOON, EASTERN STANDARD TIME, FROM THE
hidden bunker in Wyoming, General McQuarter spoke to the nation,
one day and four hours after the nuclear destruction of the former city
of Los Angeles and two hours after the reactivating of the power grid.
Communication was still problematic and her speech was unheard
by a large portion of the country, yet it had to be given, if only for
appearances' sake.

Speaking the words crafted by the administration's best speechwriters,
from sentiments dictated by the general and the Joint Chiefs, McQuarter
did her best to sound appropriately dignified and saddened.

"My fellow Americans. It is with deep anguish that I address you
today, to share our tragic loss. We have experienced the greatest horror in
our nation's history. Attacked on two fronts by enemies yet unknown, we
are broken but not beaten. In the ashes of the city of Geffensboro, lie the
souls of some nine million Americans. From those ashes, in time, we shall
rebuild that great city, stronger and more beautiful than ever."

Behind her, the men and women gathered in uniform and civilian
staffers put their hands together at the blatantly contrived applause line
and she continued.

"Our cities in the Northeast have been damaged, but not beyond repair. Boston, Chicago, Philadelphia and our nation's capital, Washington, DC shall rise again!" More applause.

"And, as if these dual tragedies were not enough, my fellow countrymen and women, I have the unpleasant duty to bring you more sad news. For the ninth time in our nation's history, a president of the United States has expired in office. Our beloved Commander-in-Chief Sarah Kate Silverman has passed away from an aneurism during the day after the attack. The very best physicians in the world could not save her. I myself held her hand in mine, as her beautiful spirit left this world. Let us have a moment of silence in memory of this great American patriot."

"What a bunch of bullshit," spoke Nicky, alone with Johnny in his office, as they watched on his seventy-five inch flat screen TV. "Gotta hand it to that fuckin' general, man. She puttin' on a good show, ain't she? Almost as good as that Meryl Stripe."

"Streep," Johnny corrected him.

"Yeah, whatever the fuck."

Johnny nodded and listened as she resumed.

"For the time being, myself and the Joint Chiefs of Staff will be in charge. I promise you, before this time tomorrow, power will be returned to each and every American home and business. I am in constant touch with the Pentagon and every effort is being made, as I speak, to uncover the rocks that hide the dirty cowards who perpetrated this horror on our country. I give you my solemn oath that they will be found. We shall hunt them down…and, to a man, or woman, they shall be destroyed!"

Applause and cheering could be heard from border to border, and sea to shining sea. Allowing a beat for the applause and cheers to die down, she concluded, her voice rising as she said, "May God bless you…and God bless the United States of America!"

"Enough a' that bull shit," said Nicky, stretching out the last two words as he pressed the off button on his remote. "Now Johnny, everybody got something to do, and I got something I need you to do for me. You and the colored boy."

Johnny cringed at the old time term for his friend's ethnicity, but he understood that Nicky was a man of the old ways. He meant no malice, but nothing anyone might say could make him join the march to modernity. In the short time he'd known Pete Holman, though, he'd come to hold him in as much esteem as any white man, and more, in fact, than most of those. It was just the old habits of nomenclature that he found himself unable to change. There were still those of his dwindling generation in the deep south who would never allow a black man to sleep in their guest room. But Nicky Santoro hadn't thought twice about having Pete as his houseguest. The man was his nephew's friend, and that was good enough for him.

"I need you two boys to go take that little girl home to see to her mama. An' while you there, make a little side trip for me."

Johnny saw what was coming. Years before, when he was twenty years old, there'd been an automobile accident, involving Tony Calabrese, in which a daughter of New Orleans high society had lost her life. Calabrese was then just beginning his career in politics, and, in order to protect his rising star, Nicky asked Johnny to testify that he'd been driving. For his loyalty, he wound up doing three years of a five-year sentence for manslaughter, paroled for good behavior, thanks to certain of Nicky's friends on the parole board.

While serving his sentence at Dixon Correctional Institute, a medium security facility in Jackson, Louisiana, north of Baton Rouge, Johnny was housed in a cellblock alongside other Santoro associates. There, his cooking skills were put to good use and his guitar playing made him leader of the prison band. Needless to say, he was able to sleep peacefully without having to worry about being assaulted sexually during his period of incarceration.

During those three years, he had occasion to observe what can happen to a young, good looking boy like himself late at night. The dark, dead eyes of those without the kind of protection Johnny enjoyed, told the story of late-night gang rapes or being the virtual sex slave of a powerful predator, for "protection" during the duration of one's time behind bars. No, being a Santoro was Johnny's salvation on the inside.

Still, three years out of a young man's life is three years and upon his release, Johnny Santoro was "owed" and thus protected, for life. However, he could expect to be called upon one day to serve. And now, that day had come.

"You remember them old boys up in New York? The young ones they got up there today is a fucking joke. That goddamn peacock Gotti ruined Brooklyn, and the rest of his old crew ain't worth dog shit neither. All they do is sniff that stuff instead of sellin' it like they supposed to be. Our only hope is Vito up in Harlem. He's gettin' up there in years but he still sharp as a tack and the ones under him know it and listen to him at least."

He was referring to Vito Gennaro, head of one of the "five families" of New York's *La Cosa Nostra*. Nicky took a sip of his *grappa* and continued, "He still in the same house, up there on 116th Street off Pleasant Avenue. You remember it. I'll Skootch his ass and let him know you'll be by to see him. Don't say nothing in his house. Feds probably got a wire on him. When you talkin' something important, go for a walk, in that park down the street."

"Thomas Jefferson Park?"

"Yeah, that's the one. I'll tell you what to say. Memorize it, don't write nothin' down. Don't call him, just go to Rao's on the corner in the afternoon and tell Frankie who you are and he'll go tell them at the door to expect you. You got all this?"

"Yeah, Nicky," Johnny nodded, "I got it."

"Okay, I already told Vito I want something done about what happened to Paulette's mama. He runs things all the way up the line through the Bronx, up into Westchester and on to Bridgeport. From there, it's Patriarca's bunch, up past New Haven and Providence to the pieces of Boston them stinky Irish don't run. So, by the time you get there, he'll know who done what to that lady, and trust me, it'll be handled. Those little mother fuckers. But I want you there to see with your own eyes when the deal goes down."

It was getting dark and Johnny was starting to fade, but the old man was still going strong, energized by a purpose he hadn't known in years.

"Now Pete, I was talkin' to him this morning, and he knows the right people in his part of town. We got to include the soul brothers if this thing gonna go right. I want him on it, like stink on shit. Take him with you. You all drive up but be careful. Take the girl's car. Her Connecticut plates won't stand out. You don't know if the airport is working up there. People gonna be nuts out there until things get straightened out. Tony tell me they sent out the National Guard and the fucking Marines too, with orders to shoot to kill any looters or punks who look sideways."

Having finally run out of instructions, he thought to give them a night on the town and said, "Look, why don't you all go over to town tonight, have something to eat, and then get you a nice rest. You gonna need it."

There were still three outstanding old school Italian restaurants in New Orleans: Café Giovanni on Rue Decatur, Liuzza's on Bienville, a favorite of Johnny's, and Pascal's Manale on Napoleon Avenue. When Pete heard the words "home of the original barbecue shrimp," their decision was made and off they went.

Unlike Italian eating establishments in other cities, where one might hear an unending barrage of Sinatra, Tony Bennett and Jerry Vale on the sound system, Pascal's featured jazz. At lunchtime, one might hear home-town heroes, like the two Louis's: Armstrong and Prima. Evening dining required something more soft and soothing, which might include ballads by soul jazz masters such as Gene Ammons, Hank Crawford or Eddie "Lockjaw" Davis.

The food was red sauce, Southern Italian. Paulette chose the veal scallopini with a side of green beans fried in butter and garlic, while Johnny went with the gnocchi in marinara sauce and a large meatball on the side. Pete knew what he wanted without looking at the menu. "I'll have your famous barbeque shrimp please, and can I get a side of bowties with red sauce?" The wait staff, recognizing Johnny as one of the Santoro clan, gave extra attentive service and the meal itself was perfect as well.

No one drank this night. The drive, non-stop, was going to be hard enough, roughly twenty-one hours. With pit stops and the three of them switching off, they could make the trip in under twenty-four. For dessert, Paulette had tiramisu and an espresso; Pete had a cannoli and a thin slice of the lightest cheesecake he ever tasted. Johnny, never a fan of mixing cheese and sugar, settled for gelato, one scoop each of vanilla and chocolate. The owner refused payment, so Johnny left a tip under his plate that was generous, yet not so much as to be insulting or seem condescending.

Back at Nicky's, the three settled in for a good night's sleep. Paulette and Johnny, too full to even think about sex, fell off into a deep slumber. The gelato, Johnny's method of preventing *agita* or, as he liked to claim, performed its function of "settling the stomach."

Dreams came to both as they slept, dreams so dark and terrible that their bodies were frozen in place. At first, Johnny's were deeply sad ones. Family and friends were gone, and there would be no more Dodger Stadium and Vin Scully, no more Langer's and their world-class pastrami, no more Santa Monica Pier with its colorful, noisy and ancient merry-go-round, no more Hollywood sign or Capitol Records Tower. His grown children's futures cut short, along with whatever their contributions to the world at large might have been.

For Paulette, even in her dream state she was unable to visualize the assault her mother had endured. There was only a blank blackness, and the sounds of the imagined screams from the woman who gave her life. After what seemed in their nightmares like hours, there was only silence. Around 3am, she awoke and, seeing him peacefully asleep at last, raised up on her elbows and, watching him in the moonlight that drifted in through the window, she leaned in to kiss his cheek and wondered what it was that made her feel the things she was beginning feel toward this much older man. She had never before been with a man even half his age. But as she lay there, watching her unlikely lover breathe, the "why" faded from her thoughts, until only the feelings remained.

He slowly opened his eyes and let the dim light reveal the beauty of her flawless skin. He ran his fingers through her hair and, taking in her scent, kissed her soft lips. She kissed him back, at first gently and then with building passion, she climbed on top of him and they made sweet love, in that way that only lovers do.

CHAPTER 11

TYPICAL OF THEIR ILK, DEMOCRATS AND Republicans from both the Senate and the House elbowed their way in front of any camera or microphone in sight to claim credit for the return of electricity. They did this mostly by subtle inference, so as to have a fallback position in the event that whoever the true hero was should come forth.

To voters, or whatever remained of the population who still went to the polls on Election Day, it didn't much matter who was responsible for the return of their refrigeration and lights, just so long as they came back on. In the most recent 2020 presidential election, voter turnout had been at an all-time low, estimated at some 11% of registered voters, of which Sarah Silverman had received not even close to half, when you included candidates from other parties. This meant that, out of a total electorate of some 260,000,000 people of voting age, only something like 15,600,000 members of the population had elected the most powerful person on the planet, a stand-up comedian whose opponent had been an obscure red state senator whose name no one could recall the day after the polls closed. Such was the name value of a B-list celebrity in an age when even minor celebs were worshiped as virtual gods.

In the aftermath of the attacks on America's second largest city and one fourth of the nation's electrical infrastructure, politicians carried little weight and no one much missed President Silverman, if they even noticed her absence. People in the northeastern states had their own problems and just wanted to be told what to do at this juncture. All they wanted from a government they no longer trusted was that things return to normal, whatever "normal" was to be from this day forth.

For those whose TVs and computers still functioned after the power surge, there were now unfamiliar faces on their screens, people mostly in military garb, offering the kinds of platitudes and slogans that bureaucrat speechwriters churned out in reams. No one paid much attention, as their main concerns were finding food and water, and cleaning up the damage caused by looters and burglars.

In Old Greenwich, servants carried out these tasks. Patricia was on her way to physical recovery. Emotional recovery would take a great deal longer. Janie's duties did not leave her much time to mourn the passing of her beloved husband, which was a blessing in disguise, for the couple had been unusually close, having been together all their adult lives, in service to two generations of the de Saint Marie family as had been Janie's parents to an earlier one.

Michelle was not much help but did the best one could expect of her. There were no more drugs and little alcohol in the house, so there was that at least, and the experience of seeing what had been done to her mother and the home she was born into brought a new seriousness to the girl, however temporary. How long this would last was anybody's guess.

At that very moment, on the New Jersey side of the Hudson River, the white BMW was waiting in line to cross the George Washington Bridge into northern Manhattan. For this final leg of their journey, Pete was at the wheel, as he was more familiar with the New York metropolitan area than either Johnny or Paulette, having spent the majority of his life between Harlem and White Plains.

"Do you want me to head up to Connecticut," he asked, "or should we stop off and see if we can catch Nicky's friend first?"

"If you can wait, Paulette, it might be more helpful if we talk to Vito and see if he's got any info yet on who did this to your mom. It'd save us a trip back."

"I agree, the traffic on the New England Thruway can be awful any time of day," she replied, "We won't want to make that trip twice in one day."

With that, Pete headed east on the Cross Bronx Expressway to the Harlem River Drive and drove south, exiting the FDR at 116th Street.

"Want me to go directly there, Johnny?"

"No, it's too early to hit Rao's." The restaurant's owner always spent each morning at local markets, purchasing the freshest meat, fish and vegetables for the evening's customers. "Cut over to 118th and First Avenue. Patsy's will be open for lunch and Drita will be there. We can have a slice and see if she'll call Frankie on his cell."

East Harlem had shrunk in size over the years, but what remained was still a highly insular Italian neighborhood, bounded by Spanish Harlem to the south and black Harlem to the north and west, past Park Avenue. Affluent whites had begun moving in a decade or more earlier, raising the rents and pushing out the area's traditional ethnic groups, except for what remained of the small section populated by the stubborn southern Italians.

Although it had been ages since they'd seen each other, Drita greeted Johnny with a tight squeeze and a warm smile. After she took their order, Johnny, pulling her close, asked, "Can you call Frankie for me? I need to see Vito."

"I can call Vito myself, babe. We deliver now, so I got the house number."

Before they'd finished their large pie, four slices plain and two with sausage for Johnny, Drita brought her cell phone to the table so he and the big man could speak.

"Hey, rock'n'roll star. I heard you was comin'. When you're done with your pie, get over here. And bring me two sandwiches, one for Tommy. She knows what we like."

Twenty minutes later, the white Beemer was parked in front of Vito's house, where there were always empty spaces waiting. This was the safest block in the city. You could leave a Rolls Royce with the doors unlocked and the windows open without fear of it being stolen, any time of day or night.

The house was a four-story brownstone, built in the late 1800s, when Harlem was designed as a suburban respite for the upper classes. But land speculators' high hopes were soon dashed as the area quickly became overbuilt and despite shining examples of "modern" architecture, such as Strivers' Row on 139th Street, designed by the famed architect Stanford White.

As land prices fell, once-fancy homes were turned into tenements and, by the 1920s, Harlem had become the "Negro Capital of the World" and 125th Street its main stem. In desperation, houses which couldn't be sold were divided into apartments and rented, at inflated prices to "less desirable" elements. Eastern European Jews moved in large numbers up from the Lower East Side into the swampy lowlands of Central Harlem between 125th Street and the northern border of Central Park, to the south.

During the 1930s, Cuban and Puerto Rican immigrants moved into parts of East Harlem, causing many blacks to move west and north, along St. Nicholas and Lennox Avenues, and south into Little Russia, pushing many of the Jews across the Harlem River where they populated the area surrounding the Grand Concourse in the Bronx.

Each of these groups was very territorial and formed street gangs to protect their turf. The earliest of these was the Canary Island gang, organized to keep any non-Irish groups from venturing west of 8th Avenue to the neighborhood known by that name. The main black gangs of that era were the Dragons and the Viceroys, each controlling separate sections of Central Harlem. East Harlem was the territory of the Red Wings, whose main rivals were the Fordham Baldies and the Golden Guineas, both across the river in the Bronx.

Unlike today, gang fights, then known as "rumbles" or "be-bopping," were fought with chains, baseball bats, switchblade knives or, at most, homemade zip-guns, nothing like the high-powered weapons in the arsenals of today's street gangs, which are more about selling drugs than protecting ethnic turf.

The Harlem Red Wings were multi-generational. The gang's membership still contained a number of men well over 50 years of age. "Once a Red Wing, always a Red Wing," the saying went, although some evolved into more respectable lines of work, like law enforcement or restaurant or shop ownership. One guy even moved to Hollywood, doing well in the motion picture business. A few others graduated to organized crime, under the auspices of Don Vito Gennaro.

From the outside, his building looked like any other Harlem brownstone. Once inside, Paulette's eyes widened at the sight of floors and walls made of rare imported Italian marble and the costly, ostentatious Louis XIV furnishings. The interior was as luxurious as that of any man of great wealth, albeit expressed in spectacularly vulgar taste. Tommy Annunziato, Vito's right hand man, led the three to his boss in the kitchen, his preferred room in which to conduct business or meet with friends. The fancier part of the house was the bailiwick of his wife, Cecile. One of his great grandchildren sat on the floor at his feet, playing quietly with a toy fire truck.

"I hope these sandwiches are still hot. I'm hungry as a lion." He fed a small piece of sauce-covered bread from the tip of his finger into the child's mouth to teethe on.

Unlike Nicky Santoro, Gennaro never used profanity in front of women. Nor did he allow its use within the walls of his home. This did not mean he was any less lethal. He offered his guests some hard candies imported from Italy and some *biscotti*, but they declined. "Then let's take a walk," he proposed.

With the child in his arms, he and Johnny led the way down Pleasant Avenue, past the old high school to Thomas Jefferson Park while Pete,

Paulette and Tommy Annunziato followed, far enough behind so as not to hear what was being said.

"Can we talk in front of them?"

"I trust Pete with my life," Johnny replied.

"And the girl?"

"Her mother's the one we're talking about, so yeah, she's okay too."

"Alright, so here's what my guys found. The ones who did the deed are from Port Chester. We know where to find them. There's maybe twenty, max. Small time punks. The town up there has changed. Turned Spanish. The niggers are not a factor, but the Spics still answer to us because we supply the dope they sell. We could have them whack the moolies and keep us out of the picture. But Nicky wants it to come from us, to send a message. I'll make it happen. Just know, my main guys have been busy, with all this shit after the grid. You think he'd be happy if I sent some of the Red Wings to do them instead? You know them guys. They can be trusted to do the job right."

"They're fine with me. Nicky wants the one called Tupac hit. No compromise on that. The others, as long as they can't retaliate, now or in the future, whatever you want to do is fine. I think your idea sounds like the way to go, Vito. When do you think her people will be safe?"

"I can get the Wings started on it tonight. Four, five days tops."

"Nicky told me to make the decision myself, so I say let's do this thing. Thank you for everything Don Vito. Nicky wants you to know he appreciates it."

"I'm gonna send Tommy up there with you." He turned and signaled to Annunziato, who ran up. "Get ahold of Ray and follow Johnny. Take your car. Watch over things and do whatever needs to be done."

Ray Annunziato was Tommy's younger brother, and both men couldn't have been more different from one another. While Ray was a practitioner of the marshal arts and in tip-top physical condition, Tommy, the type of man most other Italians would characterize as a *cafone*, but never to his face, weighed in at close to 300 pounds but was light on his feet and quick with his hands. He was known and feared for his unique ability to pluck the eyeball from an adversary's socket in the time it took for a threat to be implied.

Like Nicky, Vito was in his 90s and so was grooming his man Tommy to one day take charge. To that end, he gave him more and more latitude to make decisions on his own from time to time and, hopefully, learn from his mistakes, which were becoming fewer and fewer as time passed and his sophistication grew.

Back at the house, Ray had arrived by the time they returned from their walk and they were ready to go. Kissing both cheeks, Vito hugged Johnny and said, "Now you come see me when this thing is done. I wish I could go along, but I'm an old man." He whispered so his wife couldn't hear, "My fucking prostate's the size of a god damn *bocce* ball and I gotta get up five times a night to piss."

Johnny grinned and everyone got in their cars, Ray adding Paulette's address to his GPS in case he lost sight of the lead car, and off they went.

CHAPTER 12

THE BEST MINDS OF THE FBI, CIA AND THE MYRIAD of other alphabet intelligence entities, for all their expertise, informants and other contacts, were as yet unable to determine which of America's many enemies was responsible for either the bombing or the loss of power. At the top of the list of usual suspects were Russia, North Korea, China, Iran, and the dozens of Islamic terror organizations around the world. Typically, Iran denied any culpability, while the others usually tended to boast, which would rule out these latter, as there'd been no cyber chatter heard from them as yet. Some suspected the powerful Mexican drug cartels, with their ever-growing ubiquity.

Once the shock wore off, the American public would soon demand reprisal. However, as no one was taking responsibility, the question was, where and upon whom to retaliate? And, without retaliation, brutal retaliation, what was to prevent acts like these from happening again?

With the recent advances of smaller and more efficient methods of transporting nuclear weapons without detection, virtually any mad man with enough money and means, could place a dirty bomb in position to destroy a large city. Rogue nations, such as Russia, Pakistan and Iran, were selling the technology and components to anyone with the price of admission.

Those with eyes to see had known for decades that there were any number of scenarios in which an American city could be wiped off the map for a lifetime or more by a bomb that needed no guided missile to deliver it. By the year 2021, there were over 3000 tons of weapon-grade nuclear materials secreted away in some fifty countries. That is the equivalent of over 50,000 bombs equal in size to the one that erased the Japanese city of Hiroshima in 1945.

Given the laxity of the country's border control, it would be nothing to smuggle a weapon of that size into the United States. Even had Donald J. Trump's much-derided wall been built, a simple tunnel was all that would be needed to slip it under and through. A bomb the size of ten-kilotons would be a mere seven feet long and weigh around 1000 pounds. It could be brought in by sea, via container ship. To open and inspect every container on every ship entering either San Diego harbor or San Pedro would be impossible. Given the vast amounts of narcotics and human cargo smuggled across the 2000 miles of our southern border, to think that a box less than ten feet in length would be discovered by the Border Patrol was pure fantasy.

And none of the above includes the ability of a North Korea, which had warheads of 250 kilotons, or a Russia or China, which had Tsar Bomba of 100 megatons, which, once exploded in the air, were capable of triggering a 1600-foot-high radioactive tsunami that could destroy the entire coastline of California and any humans for miles inland.

Then there was the matter of the power grid. Wiser heads had been warning, and unheard, for more than a decade of the possibility, even likelihood, of an enemy or merely some angry kid with a laptop committing just such an act. The pundits were written off as paranoid cranks, and no fewer than four consecutive Democratic and Republican administrations had chosen to ignore the threat, until it actually happened.

The nation remained in shock. After a few days, the shock began to wear off and speculation began to run amok. The usual finger pointing and conspiracy theories from the usual paranoiacs abounded. From some corners, it was an inside job to take down the first female president. From the other side, it was a government plot to take total control of our lives. Opinion shows on CNN, Fox and MSNBC turned into hour-long shout fests, with guests talking so loudly over each other that, even had one intelligent thought emerged from the pack, it would never have been heard.

A poorly educated and mal-informed citizenry turned even more so as rumors spread like wildfire and became established "fact." On social media, Facebook and Twitter, idiocy ruled. A sober-minded person could only read the newsfeed and wonder what had ever become of common sense. For years now, the thinking few had come to see that the wildest supposition could, in a matter of moments, become accepted "truth" through repetition on the various social media. The new mantra for those increasingly few who, like Johnny Santoro "thought for themselves," was to "Believe nothing."

What other choice was there? When all sides were lying to you, where could you find a truth upon which to base your actions?

These questions and many more were being debated aboard Air Force One by the leaders of the mightiest fighting force the world had ever known, hoping to find plausible answers to convince an anxious public that their government had things under control. One thing all agreed upon was that the illusion that everything was going to be all right was more important, for the moment at least, than the actual facts, which were dismal.

In Paris, at Charles de Gaulle Airport, Jacques de Saint Marie boarded an Air France flight to JFK International in New York. He placed his carry-on in the compartment above his seat in the first-class section and, upon sitting down, fastened his seat belt and rang for a flight attendant to bring him a glass of sherry.

CHAPTER 13

PAULETTE NEEDED NO GPS TO NAVIGATE HER WAY among the winding streets of Old Greenwich. The streets in that bastion of Old Money had been purposely designed and constructed in such a way so as to confuse and discourage unwanted outsiders. Having spent the entirety of her nineteen years there, she knew every nook and cranny and every short cut in town.

It was with great relief that she pulled into the long gravel driveway of her family home. Her relief was tarnished by a fear of what she might find behind the old thick, wooden front door. Her mother had been through a trauma no one should have to endure, a horror that affected the whole family, as well as the servants. So, it was with great trepidation that she turned the key and opened the door of the large, late 19th century stone house overlooking the Long Island Sound.

She entered the only home she had ever known quietly, followed by Johnny and Pete, along with Tommy and Ray Annunziato bringing up the rear. She showed the men to the library and asked them to wait there while she went upstairs to the master bedroom, where she found her mother sitting in an alcove, staring out the window at the large red, yellow and bronze leaves that were falling from the maple trees in the back yard. Patricia always loved looking at the changing colors of the foliage in autumn. She watched as one gray squirrel chased another down the trunk of the tall, 100-year old oak that stood near the rear property line. It was the time of year when the furry, bushy-tailed creatures buried acorns in the ground, hiding them to eat during the coming winter.

"Mother," Paulette said, and Patricia turned to her daughter, as if awakened from a dream. It took a moment to register the presence of her middle child. And then she stood and the two fell tearfully into each other's arms.

"Are you all right Mommy?"

"I will be, dear. And you? You must have been so worried. Where have you been?"

Deftly changing the subject, she replied, "Mother, I've brought some friends. They want to help. They're going to stay with us a few days if that's all right with you."

"If that's what you want, darling, why yes, of course."

"It is what I want, and when you're ready I'd like for you to come down and meet them." She looked around the room where her mother had been brutally attacked, just a few days before, shuddering as she tried not to picture the scene as it took place.

"They're not the kind of people you're used to, so please don't be alarmed. These are good men who have been very kind to me."

"Of course, dear. Just give me some time to wash up and put on something nice to wear. And ask Cook to please make something for your friends to eat. You all must be so very hungry."

Paulette did as she was told and, assuming her sister was in her room and did not wish to be disturbed, passed by her door and returned to the library.

In her absence, the men had been discussing plans for the coming confrontation with Patricia's attackers. They'd been out of contact with Vito for an hour and were wondering when it was going to go down. Johnny also needed access to Wi-Fi, so he could safely speak with Nicky and bring him up to date. All talk ceased when Paulette entered the room.

"Come on guys, I'm a part of this too. After all we've been through together, are you going to leave me out in the cold? It's not fair," stopping as she caught the slight whine in her voice.

"It's not about fairness, Paulette," said Johnny, "It's about your safety. Things are going to happen soon that it's better you know nothing about. What I need right now is Wi-Fi and some privacy."

A servant brought beverages on a tray and plates of sandwiches cut in quarters with the crusts removed and piled in an artful pyramid, while Paulette took Johnny and Tommy up to her room so they could use his laptop there in private. Tommy grabbed two of the tiny sandwiches and a ginger ale on the way out, leaving Pete and Ray to get better acquainted.

With both Nicky and Vito on Skootch, Vito began the conversation and informed the others that the Red Wings had scoped out the basement headquarters where Tupac Prentiss and his crew met most nights. It was in one of those old, narrow three-story wooden row houses, the kind that were one to one and a half rooms wide and two or three rooms deep from front to back on the bottom two floors, with a single attic bedroom on the third. The buildings on either side were built from exactly the same floor plan and a very few feet apart. In the basement the gang used as a sort of clubhouse, would be a furnace and a hot water heater that served the entire building. There was one lone entrance to the basement from the stairs in the hall, along with an old unused coal shoot outside on the right side of the house that could provide a possible escape route for someone as small as Prentiss.

One shooter would be stationed on the roof of each adjoining building and four men would watch the front door from a van across the street, while another three would guard the back door. The plan called for one of the Red Wings to toss a grenade down the shoot and the others would wait as their prey fled for the hills at the sound of the explosion.

Nicky liked the plan and reminded Johnny that he wanted him to be on hand to verify when Tupac met his maker. They disconnected and went back downstairs to the library.

All was now set for the following night. Except for one thing. From his experience as a Navy Seal during the Gulf War, Pete felt it best to reconnoiter in advance so as to be fully aware of all possible escape routes in case of any unplanned-for problems. Although he understood and accepted that this was Vito's show, his military training told him that it would be best if it were planned out as an op with more specific roles for each man. The others agreed to the reconnoiter and got up to leave.

But Paulette insisted on accompanying them. "…not because I have any desire to be there when you go. I just want to see with my own eyes where you'll be." So, the five of them piled into Tommy's big black Lincoln Town Car and headed to Port Chester.

CHAPTER 14

AROUND 11 AM THE NEXT MORNING, AN AIRPORT limousine delivered Jacques to his home and family. After introductions all around, Johnny suggested he and the guys should go out for a bite to eat for a couple hours so the family could have some time alone.

After a light lunch, Tommy and Ray sat at the bar to calm their nerves, leaving Johnny and Pete in a booth to talk.

"Did you see that ring Jacques was wearing, Johnny?"

"No, why?"

"It was a Freemason ring. I know that because my aunt was an Eastern Star and her ring had the same insignia. Now, I get it."

"So? Now, you get what?"

"Dude, he's been playing Nicky. He knew all along what Nicky was looking for, and I'd bet the farm he wants the same thing, only he wants to make sure Nicky's on the level before he commits."

"Which means what?"

"I have dozens of books on Freemasonry, the history, all the way back to the 15th century. The Knights of Templar, the Illuminati, all that shit. You think the Mafia is a big deal? These motherfuckers oversee a thousand times more and have for centuries. I mean, dude, U.S. presidents have been Freemasons. Back to George Washington, James Monroe, both Roosevelts,

Harry Truman, fucking Gerald Ford, man. Benjamin Franklin, even! Don't nothing get past these cats."

"What are you saying? That Jacques has known all along that Nicky wants the Freemasons to join up with the mob as a way of getting back the power they lost in the '70s?"

Pete snapped his fingers three times and said, "Never doubt old Pete, baby. If I tell you it's gonna rain, you better bring your galoshes."

He took out a one-dollar bill and laid it on the table and turned it over. "See that eye on top of the pyramid there? That's the Eye of Providence, the all-seeing eye of God. Those thirteen steps on the unfinished pyramid? They represent the original thirteen states. The message in Latin at the bottom is *Novus Ordo Seclorum* or 'New World Order.' Sound familiar? Some of these dudes signed the Declaration of Independence *and* the Constitution of the United States."

"Aw, come on, Pete. That's crazy talk."

"I'm telling you, man. Dig this: The street design in the nation's capital was laid out by this French cat, Pierre Charles L'Enfante in 1791. Cat was a Freemason, and it's designed in that upside-down star, man. Masonic symbols are all over the place in that town. Everywhere you look."

"Shit, I don't know. What's it all mean?"

"It means this. If Nicky and his peeps, and Jacques and his bunch get together, they're gonna rule the whole god damn world. Won't be no stopping 'em."

"Jesus Fucking Christ! You think?"

"Yeah, and who says they don't already? Or at least the Masons? You know how you always saying both political parties are full of shit and that's why you're an independent? A card-carrying cynic, like you always say? Well you're onto something, man, and you don't even know it. Check this out: Right now, the Democrats are in power, right?"

"Yeah."

"Before that, it was the Republicans, and before that you had the Democrats. It's like a fucking pendulum, man, always back and forth. The Republicans promise lower taxes but they never deliver. Voters get pissed, so they elect Democrats, who promise lots of free shit, neglecting to inform the people there ain't no such thing as 'free.' Takes four or eight years and they get wise and vote their ass out of office and the bullshit starts all over again. Back and forth, back and forth, every four to eight years. People are stupid. They get their opinions from bumper stickers. They vote for the guy with the best haircut or the best line of shit. They fall for it every time, voting for the "D" or the "R" like Pavlovian dogs, depending on which tribe they belong to. They think they're voting for 'change.' But there ain't never no change; it's just more of the same old same old."

"I can't argue that."

"Damn right you can't. Cause you know I'm right, brother. Look what we've had. Four out of the last five: Clinton, Obama, Trump and Silverman. All slick-talkin' professional bullshit artists. Ol' W, he worked that good ol' boy game, played dumb, but he was smarter than he let on. His old man was Illuminati."

"You're starting to lose me here. What are you talking about now?"

"All I'm saying is, there's basically two kinds of people in this world: ones whose actions are determined by logic and those whose actions are determined by their emotions. You see 'em out there, when they don't get their way, yelling and burning, protesting, like babies throwin' a temper tantrum. They *react*, man; they don't *think*. Show 'em a sad-eyed puppy or a little kitten and they reach for their checkbook. Give 'em a big-eyed, nappy-headed pickaninny with cancer and they'll hand over their whole god damn bank account."

"Dude, where you headed with all this?"

"Balance, man. The need for balance. Yin and yang. That's what I'm talking about."

"Man, you are out there today, I swear," he laughed uncomfortably.

"Tell you what. When we get back to the crib, let's see if we can get Jacques off by himself and get him talking. I got a feeling, if we get him to open up, he's gonna be saying some of the same shit I just told you. I'm not jivin' you, man."

Johnny just shook his head and stood up to leave.

They grabbed the Annunziato brothers, before they had too much to drink, and headed back, to rest up and prepare themselves for the night's work.

CHAPTER 15

EARLY THAT MORNING, NICKY'S NERD BOYS HAD come running to the compound gate, telling the guard they had something "super important" to tell the boss. It was the news Nicky had been hoping for: the whereabouts of the person, or persons, who hacked the grid.

In the lead-lined private room, safe from prying ears, the boys revealed that, as they'd thought, the perpetrator was in Minnesota, Minneapolis, to be precise. They traced the laptop's IP to two addresses, both in the same general area. One turned out to be a Starbucks and the other was a small apartment house on a dingy block in a working-class part of town. They said they had it pinned down to an apartment on the second floor.

"You sure?" Nicky said, his heart pounding fast with all the excitement of a big game hunter closing in on his quarry.

"Yes, absolutely; we've had him there several times, mostly late afternoons and at night. He's usually at the Starbucks during the day."

"Good work, you little fuckers. I got something nice for you when we catch his ass. Now stay put; I got a call to make."

Moments later, he was on the phone with Tony Calabrese with the good news, conveying the information in their gutter Sicilian dialect for the sake of privacy. The only question they needed to decide was, should Nicky send men to deal with the hacker, or was it better, in terms of Calabrese's political ambitions, for Tony to give the information to his contact at the

FBI, making himself the hero? By not revealing his source, he could keep Nicky out of it and appear mysterious and thus more attractive to voters.

They decided upon the latter as the better course of action. Tony immediately contacted his inside man at FBI headquarters in Washington and they set up the sting in a way that would bring favorable attention to Tony. Later, before the TV cameras, he would generously give credit to "the real heroes, America's finest, the men and women who serve and protect the citizens of this great country." Handsome Tony Calabrese could fake modesty with the best of them.

Within the half hour, he and a trusted aide were on a Delta Airlines flight from Washington to Minneapolis, having barely made it to the gate in time. Forced to sit in coach, due to the last-minute booking, they used the last few moments prior to take off to arrange for agents to pick them up at Crystal Airport and take them to the FBI's local office in nearby Brooklyn Center on Freeway Boulevard where they were to meet with the local head man, who turned out to be a woman named Lois Saunders.

Although Tony and his aide were to be positioned at a safe distance from the actual take down, they were outfitted with bullet-proof vests and helmets, mostly for show. Being rather vain about his hair, Tony hated the idea of wearing a helmet and left it off. They would be driven in one of the Bureau's black Ford SUV's used for transporting lead personnel to the command post. The actual S.W.A.T. team would arrive on scene in a heavy-duty armored vehicle, in this case a Lenco Bear Cat of the type used by most agencies and police departments. Two drones would be hovering above in an observational capacity.

In the unarmored van containing computers and other communication devices, it was determined that the suspect, who had spent the early part of the day at the Starbucks location, was in transit, likely on his way to the apartment on the second-floor rear. As the large S.W.A.T. vehicles would be hard to miss, they were parked two blocks away, until the suspect was determined to be in the house and his computer turned on. Since his face was unknown to law enforcement, the only way to know he was there was if he fired up his laptop. The building was being observed by agents, in two unmarked cars parked across the street and two agents at the back door to prevent escape. Snipers were positioned on the adjoining rooftops and the bomb squad was at the ready.

At around 3:30 pm, communications informed everyone that the suspect was in place in the house and at the computer. Plainclothes officers were dispatched to warn the other tenants to quietly vacate the building. The optimum goal was to take him or her alive in order to extract information regarding possible accomplices.

At precisely 4:04 pm, in full gear, the team battered down the door and entered the apartment, shouting "FBI! Federal agents! Face down on the floor! Hands and legs spread wide!" Seated at the computer was a young man who appeared to be in his early-to-mid 20s, red laser beams from three government-issued weapons aimed at his chest. He wore a full blonde beard and on top of his head of sandy hair he wore the white, round cap of the type worn by Muslim men called the *tagiyah* or *kufi* prayer cap. He was clearly not of Middle Eastern extraction but appeared to possibly be born of the northern European ancestry common to Minnesota: the Swedes, the Finns and the Danes. He was obviously a convert, radicalized from viewing the various Islamic terrorist sites, such as those of ISIS or Boko Haram.

Seeing the FBI insignia on their flack jackets, he moved to smash his laptop in an attempt to prevent his captors from using it to extract information, but the butt of a rifle to the head prevented him from doing so.

Suddenly, a gunshot rang from the bedroom doorway, hitting an agent in the unprotected side of his torso where his vest failed to provide cover. Another agent swirled and fired twice, hitting a freckle-faced, pale young woman holding a smoking Luger semi-automatic pistol, knocking her to the floor, blood rushing from her abdomen and chest. As she lay mortally wounded, her *hijab* fell away, revealing strands of curly red hair.

The young man tried to stand up but was again knocked to the floor. He cried *"Allah Akbar"* and an agent pounced on him, a knee pressed against his spine to hold him in place, yanking his hands behind his back and restraining him with a pair of the plastic Flexi Cuffs he carried on his belt. He was read his Miranda rights and over their radios, the team's superiors were notified of the quick and relatively easy arrest.

Tony Calabrese immediately instructed his aide to contact the local TV news and the big three cable news networks, who they'd alerted earlier that a big story was about to go down and where to be situated to assure the best maximum coverage. The TV trucks were quick to arrive, cameras, sound and lights at the ready and the city's top female reporters and network "news babes" too, hair and make-up artists in tow, all anxious to be first with the biggest scoop of the year.

They were all set up to let the cameras roll as the hacker was led out of the building, even as the bomb squad searched the apartment with bomb sniffing dogs and explosive detection devices. The suspect's chosen name was the unimaginative, almost comically rhyming Ahmed Mohammed while the name on his birth certificate and driver's license read Nils Johansson. Later that evening, when interviewed by reporters, his former high school guidance councilor would state that, as a teen, the boy had displayed "severe authority issues," while his university dean reported that he took such easy "no sweat" courses as Gender, Diversity and Social Justice Studies and various Philosophy courses, somehow managing to get failing grades in all of these.

A podium was quickly set up, with a phalanx of microphones. At this point, Senator Antonino Calabrese of Louisiana stepped forward and gave a brief speech, in the vaguely Louisiana accent he saved for when he was speaking to northern audiences, thanking "the real heroes, the patriotic men and women of the Federal Bureau of Investigation who captured this suspect, and with a minimal loss of life. Regrettably, an accomplice who surprised our agents, firing on them, had to be taken down," omitting the fact that the dead person was a young and attractive, freckle-faced American woman.

"I will not be taking questions at this time. For that, I turn you over to Special Agent in Charge Lois Saunders. This is a great day for our nation. Take it away, Agent Saunders."

Tony stepped to the side, making sure to remain within camera frame, so as to display his humility, as Special Agent Saunders spoke in that dry, practiced way law enforcement professionals have of speaking without saying anything substantial. The journalists asked the usual dumb questions, mostly repeating what previous reporters had already asked, questions designed to get their faces on camera for a few seconds longer than their rivals.

"Fucking amateurs," Calabrese chuckled to his aide, reverting back to his natural dialect, "I said ten words, and who they gonna remember? Me, mother fucker." To himself, he thought, *I'm gonna owe Nicky big time now*, and he was not wrong.

CHAPTER 16

AT HOME IN HIS STUDY, SURROUNDED BY THE oaken wainscoting halfway up the walls, and after a tearful reunion with his wife, Jacques de Saint Marie watched the arrest of the power grid hacker on CBS Breaking News and, noticing that the man at the podium was the Honorable Senator from Louisiana, gathered that Nicky Santoro was somehow involved in the discovery and/or apprehension of the young, blonde man pictured on the screen in Muslim garb. Now, even more than before, he was convinced that Santoro was a man with whom he wished to be in business. His objective from this point forward would be to concoct a situation that each man would find mutually advantageous and, more important, to construct that situation in such a way as to shield himself and his fellow Freemasons from the cagey old man's potential for trickery.

Simultaneously, back at his compound in Metairie, the old man was entertaining thoughts of a similar nature, as he viewed the lovely and brilliant Dana Perino on Fox News reporting the same story. Nicky liked her, partially because she was of Italian descent as well as for her luxurious mane of thick blonde hair that flowed onto her shoulders. Like him, she was short and had the familiar facial features of a *Paisana*. He often speculated as to whether her roots were in the north or the south of his ancestral lands, preferring to believe she was a *Napoletana*, as had been the lost love of his life, a slight, olive complected 13-year old named Angelina D'Apace who had stolen his heart when he was but 21 years of age. Her father, a thick-necked, muscle-bound shrimp fisherman named Angelo, would have none of it. He considered Nicky, or any relation of Carlos Marcello, to be *la feccia della società*, a scum of the earth and unworthy of ever penetrating his daughter's loins. He would have forfeited his life, rather than allow this man Santoro ever to enjoy the soft flesh of his only child and namesake.

Although, at age 98, it had been many years since he'd enjoyed a full erection, the sight of the petite, blonde newscaster on the 75-inch screen of his Samsung flat screen TV never failed to bring a tingle to his *cazzo*, as the ancient blood, thinned by the daily medication for his cholesterol and blood pressure, coursed through his veins and slowly flooded the old man's lifeless, low-hanging organ. With arthritic fingers, he fondled it through his loose trousers in the vain hope that Perino's beauty, the sound of her soft, aristocratic voice and the memories of his beloved Angelina and his many hard-ons past might stimulate something more than the occasional "semi" he seldom achieved these days.

At this moment, in the midst of his romantic reverie, Carmela silently padded into the room, to see if her boss needed any refreshment, and caught a glimpse of this routine that seemed to occur whenever Dana Perino appeared on the big screen TV.

"You playin' wit' yourself over that blonde news lady again, Boss? You know you too old for that mess. If you don't be careful, you gonna rub that thing right down to the nub."

"What the hell's the matter with you, woman? Sneakin' up on a man in his own room like that. I oughta knock you down."

"Shit, you jus' try and beat on me Bubba. I'll come back late at night an' cut you in you damn sleep. Shit."

"You need to watch yo' language 'round here. Show a little respect for the hand that feeds that big god damn mouth of yours."

More than fifty years of this kind of repartee came as easy as breathing for these two old friends for, more than employer/employee, friends was very definitely what they were.

Patricia quietly entered the study where Jacques sat at his desk, deep in thought. From that day they'd met at his club's tennis court, so long ago, no other man's penis had ever entered her, so much had she come to love and respect this man, the father of her children and the provider of the life she had longed for since she was but a girl. As much as she loved him, there was of course the element of gratitude, and the sense of duty to honor her marriage vows as well. For Patricia was the product of Connecticut parochial schools, educated and trained by the good nuns, in addition to having studied and learned the obligations and traditions of the society to which she had desired to belong. As often as she was left alone with her vodka in that big house, her husband away on the business that paid for all she possessed, she had known no other man and, in time, her gratitude had indeed turned to love. Until that awful night, that is, when those ugly, smelly young men—she'd lost count how many—penetrated her in the most evil, brutal ways, ways in which her Jacques could never have dreamed of.

Now, seeing him in his chair, his back to her and unaware of her presence, she wanted to reach out and touch him, to feel his warmth and strength, to feel safe again, to be reassured that he did not find her tainted, to feel once more worthy of his love, to let him know that she had never, not for one instant, felt the slightest pleasure in what those brutes had done to her. For in a way, what they did to her, they did to him and to her family as well, and, in a sense, did to all good and decent people everywhere.

They must be made to pay. And pay they would tonight, at the hands of these new friends her daughter had brought into their home. Who and what these men were did not enter into her consciousness just now. Their background was unimportant. Her only thought was that she felt protected, cared for. Honored. As that woman in that old black and white movie--Blanche was her name, Patricia thought—yes, Blanche Dubois it was. That woman had said something about "the kindness of strangers." And Patricia was comforted by the notion. The kindness of these strangers was the gift her prayers had brought to her. Perhaps vengeance would bring her peace and closure. Such a commonplace term, *closure*. It was one of those words bandied about by mediocre people, the type whose thoughts were dictated to them by the tabloid newspapers or the cheap magazine headlines beyond which people of that sort seldom if ever read.

She went to her husband and put her hands upon his shoulders, massaging the tension in the tight, tired muscles and kissing the scruffy hair on the back of his neck, catching him unaware that she'd been standing there, she, wondering if he could still accept her or if what had happened to her--to *them*--might matter, or prevent him from feeling for her as he had before. Her need to touch him finally erased any fear that he might reject her, or even cause that split second of doubt that could destroy their love. And so, she did, and her courage was rewarded as he took her hands in his and kissed each finger, one by one. He turned to her and the kindness in his eyes told her all she needed to know.

CHAPTER 17

TOMMY ANNUNZIATO READ THE CODED TEXT
that came from one of Vito's burner phones. It read, *Show cancelled tonight. Singer took ill. Come home.* He translated the words into *Tupac Prentiss can't be located. Will reschedule.*

He informed Johnny, then gathered his brother and their things and headed to East Harlem in the big black Lincoln town car. This left Johnny with the job of telling the family the raid was off for the time being. But first he Skootched this information to Nicky, who ordered him to stay put and wait to hear from Vito.

With the remainder of the afternoon and evening to themselves, Pete suggested they take a ride to White Plains to visit his mother and sister.

"Good thinking," said Johnny, "We don't want to overstay our welcome here. Plus, I love your mom."

Overhearing their conversation, Paulette offered to drive them. She was still not comfortable with the elephant of her mother's rape in the room and felt it best to give her parents some more alone time to try and begin to heal. Plus, the notion of meeting new people from a world other than her own appealed to her taste for adventure.

So, the three hopped onto the New England Thruway and drove south to the Cross Westchester Route 287 west, exiting at Tarrytown Road, heading west to Hillside Avenue, north past the former Greenburgh Junior High

School and Parkway Gardens, where upscale black families had long lived in well-kept homes. Doctors, lawyers and celebrities like Jackie "Moms" Mabley, singer LaVern Baker, comedian Slappy White and the photographer and film maker Gordon Parks all lived there once upon a time.

When they reached Old Tarrytown Road, they made a left into a tiny neighborhood of small, modest homes. A left turn, onto Warren Avenue, and another onto Oak Street and they arrived at the house where Pete Holman spent his teens, the home where his mother and sister still lived.

The unincorporated town of Greenburgh, as did the rest of Westchester County and much of southern Connecticut, contained an unusually large number of country clubs, one of which was Metropolis, where Pete had worked as a caddy when he was a teenager, one of the few of his race to be so employed there. Most of the other caddies were the rough and tumble Italian or Irish boys, like Babe Telesco, Butch Futia, Patsy Pelligrino and Eddie Murphy, whose upper arms were the size of most men's thighs. Strong for his age, Pete could make two "loops" of eighteen holes each per day. He loved golf and often came in at sunrise to play a few holes with the set of used clubs he purchased at a pawn shop on lower Main Street in White Plains. He knew every inch of the course, every sand trap and each rise in every hill and the angle of each green, making him a valuable asset to the club's golfers who, in defiance of the club's rules, always tipped him, quietly and well.

Membership at Metropolis Country Club was strictly limited to German Jews. Elmwood, just up the street, was reserved for Eastern European Jews whom the already largely assimilated Germans, having arrived in America a half century previously, looked down upon as crass, vulgar "types," with their Yiddishisms, flashy Cadillacs and loud, bejeweled wives. Those of German descent viewed their counterparts from the east as exhibiting traits which provoked anti-Semitism and therefore avoided them socially, as their goal was to assimilate deeper into the larger culture.

These Ashkenazi Russians, Poles and Hungarians could never hope to be invited to dine at Metropolis, much less be accepted as members.

Metropolis members mocked Elmwood's poorly designed course for its long, steep hill between the eighth and ninth holes which tired out the players so that many of the older men quit and spent the remainder of the afternoon in the club's bar. In the winter, the children of the neighborhood's *goyem* jumped the fence and rode their sleds down that long hill, forcing the lone, uniformed security man out of his cozy cottage to check and chase the boys back across the fence, the bigger ones throwing snowballs at him as they retreated and laughed all the way home.

Paulette's family, by contrast, was fourth generation Greenwich Country Club members. Founded in 1892 as the fourth country club established in the United States, it was, and remained, the essence of Old World luxury. The de Saint Marie clan was the first Catholic family to be awarded club membership in 1946 to honor her great grandfather's heroism in the Battle of the Bulge, and it was there on the tennis court that Patricia met the man who was to become her husband. No longer completely "exclusive," there have been two Italian board presidents since the year 2000, and a very select few Jewish members. Club membership has long included many world leaders in business, finance and government.

Pete's high school, Woodlands, was built on 190 acres of the former Warburg estate, which had once encompassed some 500 acres of prime real estate adjacent to Metropolis Country Club, both owned by one Felix M. Warburg, the fabulously wealthy German-Jewish banker in the early 20th Century. In pre-income tax America, Warburg was able to amass a kingly fortune, allowing himself and his wife Frieda Schiff Warburg to become two of New York's premier philanthropists, dividing their time between their mansion at 1109 Fifth Avenue at 92nd Street, their home in Palm Beach, Florida and the estate in Greenburgh, which boasted fully stocked stables, tennis courts, numerous out dwellings and a stream-fed swimming pool, complete with its own small, sandy, man-made beach.

All these dwellings were filled with the rare European furniture and art of the kind found in the homes of the Old Money WASP culture which he, and especially his wife, aspired to emulate.

All this minutia came up in conversation during the half hour drive from Greenwich to Greenburgh and by the time they got to the little house on Oak Street all were fully informed of each other's country club background.

Pete's mother and sister had gone all out cooking a soul food dinner of his favorites: breaded chicken cutlets, home fries, mac'n'cheese, collard greens, green peas, corn bread, biscuits and gravy, blueberry cobbler and the apple pie for which Betty Holman was locally famous. His sister Carole had watched her mother bake it a thousand times and, for the life of her, could not get it to taste the same. Betty claimed her secret ingredient was love. If pressed, she would hint that it was also the fact that she used "more butter than the law allows." For her piecrust, as well as her cookies, she'd somehow discovered the secret of just how much butter could be packed into a recipe without causing the crust to fall apart. Every woman in the area marveled at her skill as a baker.

Betty's taste in singers ran to the great black baritone balladeers of the past, Nat "King" Cole, Billy Eckstine, Arthur Prysock and Lou Rawls. Whenever Pete was on the road and wandered into a music store or thrift shop that sold CDs or LPs, he'd look for one of her favorites and mail it home to her with a pretty card, on which he signed "I love you Mom, Your boy Pete." On the stereo at the moment was one of these, the rich, deep sound of Rawls singing "If I Were A Magician."

After dinner, Paulette asked to see the room where Pete kept his famous collection of books. "Oh! My! God! You've read all these?" she said as her eyes took in the stacks containing many millions of words and the wisdom of the ages.

"Every word," Pete nodded and smiled. Like many a proud and loving mother, Betty kept his bedroom just as he'd left it, so it could be ready for her son whenever he was in town.

It was the first time in her young life that Paulette had been in such close proximity to a black family who were not employed by her own. While she recognized the same warmth and tenderness she knew so well from her former nannie, Janie, this was somehow different, more relaxed, more natural and unforced. She instantly loved the closeness she felt in this home and wanted to experience more of that feeling in her own life.

Intuitively, she understood that she had entered someone else's world, *their* turf, *their* home court. and was experiencing, first hand, how black people interacted with each other when not on the outside, "performing" for whites. In her culture, the attributes of kindness and compassion for "the Other" were encouraged, in school, by the media and under peer pressure, but for the first time in her life, she was seeing, with her own eyes and heart, that hanging out with your cool black friends at a party or a club was something entirely different than this. That was performance art, this was real, human-to-human, familial contact and interaction, on a level few in the society at large ever experienced.

"Do you have a picture of your mother, Johnny?" asked Betty. "I don't think I've ever seen what she looked like."

His mom had passed away some years before and he kept a number of photos of her at various ages on his iPhone. He showed them around.

"Oh my! She was quite a beauty, wasn't she? In this one shot, she must be around Paulette's age. I see a resemblance, don't you Carole?"

Carole took the phone and said, "Yes, definitely. I can't tell, but she looks a little blonde here. Was she?"

Johnny replied, "She was, yes, but not as much as it looks in this picture. It must be the lighting, the reflection of the sun on her hair. Her people were from the north, Torino, I think, but I'm not sure. She never talked about it. This caused some minor problems, at first among my dad's family.

They're Sicilian and they don't get along with northern Italians. But eventually they accepted her."

Pete chimed in, "Dude, black people are like that too. My daddy said when we first moved up to Harlem from the south, people called him 'country' and made fun of his clothes, his shoes and his Alabama accent."

"Oh my Lord," laughed Betty, "The first thing colored people look at is the shoes. Always, the shoes."

"Yeah," said Carole, "But with black people, it's even more about skin color. 'If you're white, you're all right. If you're yellow, you're mellow. If you're brown, turn around. If you're black, get back.'"

She and Pete laughed, but Betty was uncomfortable. She was of a generation that considered it unwise to expose your private weaknesses in the presence of white people. She could barely use the word *Negro*, much less *black*. The *au courant* term *African-American* made her a nervous wreck.

"Well, I still say, there's a strong resemblance to Paulette," she interjected. "You know what they say, a man always chooses a girl who's like his mama."

"Oh Mom, please, you're going to embarrass them," said Carole. "They don't need a matchmaker," wondering to herself about the vast age difference, and projecting down the line about the likely problems to come if this should turn out to be more than a mere fling.

To change the subject, Pete asked about this person or that neighbor and got an earful of local gossip. At one point, Paulette felt comfortable enough to ask, "What did your dad do?"

It was Betty who replied. "My husband Bill, he was a handy man. Self-employed. He could fix or make anything. A roof, a wall, he could install an entire bathroom, electricity and plumbing both. He even built that little house next door for my late mother. From scratch, no blueprint, no nothing. Just from his own eye. That house was all she needed, a living room, kitchen, bath and a bedroom."

Pete chimed in, "He loved to sing too. In the early fifties, he sang in two doo-wop groups from right here in White Plains, the Swans and the Master-tones. All that remains of them is the couple records they made that went nowhere. You wanna hear them?"

Paulette nodded and everyone else said yes. So, Pete went to Carole's computer and found the Master-tones' song "Tell Me" on YouTube and everyone listened in rapt silence.

"That's Willie Rat on lead vocal. You ever heard a prettier voice? Whatever happened to him, Mom?"

Betty spoke, "He went to work for the city, counseling young kids from broken homes. He's retired and living over on Battle Hill, married to that pretty light-skinned lady, Delma. The one with the good hair."

To clarify, Pete added, "Battle Hill was where George Washington fought the Battle of White Plains on October 28, 1776. Ol' George was outnumbered and forced to retreat across the Hudson River by combined British and Hessian forces."

Johnny cut in, "Dude, your mind is a warehouse of useless knowledge," and everyone laughed.

"It's that photographic memory," Betty said, smiling proudly.

Pete continued, "Man, that Willie Rat could croon, and how about Sherman, the bass singer? He still around?"

Carole said, "When General Foods opened up their building on the east side of White Plains, they hired him and put him in an office by the front door with some phony title. He called himself the HNIC: Head Negro in Charge. They gave him nothing to do and he was told to keep his door open at all times, so anybody entering the building would see they hired at least one of us."

Everyone laughed, except Paulette, who found it terribly sad. She stood up and went over to where Mrs. Holman sat in her old overstuffed armchair and squeezed in next to her and gave her a long hug. "Don't be sad, baby, that's just how it was in those days. We were happy when one of us got a job.

Remember, he was a 'first,' and a first always leads to a second and a third. Today, one of us is the head of that damn company. Excuse my French."

If anyone were to ask Paulette what attracted her to this family, all of whom were far more than twice her age, and why did she prefer their company to those in her own peer group, she'd have been unable to come up with a sufficient answer. All she knew was, she had never before felt so at ease. Friends had always told her she was born in the wrong century. She thought about how, unlike her own mother and sister, no one here was tipsy or locked away in another room, getting high. But mostly, she just enjoyed listening to the conversations and the reminiscing, her head resting on Betty's shoulder. As Arthur Prysock sang "Fly Me to The Moon," she drifted off into a contented reverie.

The conversation continued, often running off into tangents, until after midnight. Carole went off to her room and Betty told Pete, "Why don't you spend the night, honey? Johnny and his girl can sleep on the pull-out here in the living room. I'll make you all a nice big breakfast in the morning. She's a good girl, so I'll make an exception to my rule about no unmarried couples sleeping in my house. Just this once."

Pete smiled and went back to the living room to check with Johnny and Paulette while Betty pulled sheets, blankets and pillows from a linen closet, happy to have company in her home.

CHAPTER 18

IN THE MORNING, THEY AWOKE TO THE AROMA
of what promised to be a scrumptious breakfast. Carole was dressed for
work and, conscious of her weight, had only a small glass of grapefruit
juice and a bowl of oatmeal, no sugar.

For the past twenty-odd years, she'd been employed at one of the
nation's largest insurance companies, working as an executive secretary
to one of the top men at the local White Plains branch office. In the wake
of recent events, she could expect to be working many long hours for the
foreseeable future. This was the least of her problems. Claims from the
west coast and the Northeastern sector were coming in by the thousands
daily and those who knew about such things feared the company could
conceivably end up insolvent.

Although many people are under the impression that insurance is a
charity, or should be run like one, in truth, insurance is a business. And the
nature of that business is gambling, pure and simple. To fully understand
it, an insurance company should be viewed as a casino, the house, if you
will. The person purchasing a policy is betting that tragedy of one kind or
another will befall him and so, lays down his bet. The company, that is, the
house, wagers that nothing bad will happen, which, given the percentages,
is the more likely outcome. Great studies are made and actuaries are calcu-
lated to determine the likelihood of accidents or illness and the consequent

cost of premiums and deductibles that will provide the greatest profit for shareholders, as well as the most acceptable price to the customer.

Variables, such as age, location, health, personal habits and so forth are taken into consideration as well. After more than twenty years at her desk, Carole Holman knew as much as anyone about the business. So, Johnny took the opportunity to ask her a few questions.

"I've lost my house, my car and all my possessions in the LA bombing. I'm sure I've even lost my insurance agent and all my papers. I don't know what to do. Any ideas? Do you think any record of me still exists?"

Carole thought for a moment and said, "Nothing like this has ever happened before, so, like everybody else, insurance companies are trying to figure it all out. I can answer one of your questions: your information is probably stored on the Cloud or at a number of locations around the country. What company are you with?"

As it turned out, his policy happened to be with the very company she worked for.

"Great, I may be able to help. I'll put you on the top of the pile in my inbox as soon as I get to the office and keep you posted, okay?"

He threw his arms around her and said, "You're a life saver! That's a big load off my mind."

"Just don't expect any money overnight, but I'll move it along as best I can. You're family, Johnny, and that puts you at the head of the line. You gonna be okay for money in the meantime?"

"Yeah, I got my credit card and cash from my last road gig."

"Your card should still be good. Just spend as little of that cash as possible, just in case. I gotta run babe. Stay in touch. Love you." As she walked out the door, she turned around and said, "And don't worry Johnny, I got you covered."

With that concern off his shoulders, he felt a lot better. He knew Nicky would wire him money if need be and, as a last resort, Paulette's family would surely loan him something, but his motto was "Never a lender nor a borrower be," as the old saying went.

When he walked back into the kitchen, Pete and Paulette were at the table in the middle of their meal.

"Sit down, man, and check out this bacon," said Pete, "Waffles or French toast?"

Johnny looked over at Paulette's plateful of the latter and decided on that. He lifted a glass of orange juice to his lips and Betty said, "Sorry we have no fresh O.J. like you have in sunny California, baby." She caught herself, "I'm so sorry, Johnny. I wasn't thinking."

"No worries, Bett, I'll just have the French toast."

After breakfast, Pete wanted to take the car he kept in the garage for when he was off the road and go for a ride to make sure the battery was fully charged. He also wanted to check in with some of his local White Plains buddies, some of whom were in his age group, while others were somewhat younger and veterans of more recent wars than the one in which he'd served. He had a feeling he might feel a lot safer if at least a couple of them would be willing to go along to Port Chester.

He knew the Red Wings were tough customers but, unlike Vito Gennaro's regular crew, they were not killers by nature, nor by profession. True, more than one had taken the lives of enemies in battle but, as a rule, murder on demand was not their specialty. On the other hand, Pete's friends, some of whom counted themselves as Navy Seals, like himself, as well as Green Berets and Special Forces guys, were trained assassins, and proven under difficult circumstances. That is not to say they enjoyed killing; no soldier does. But when it was justified, he knew they would not hesitate if necessity demanded. And battle is one place where even a second's hesitation can get you killed.

He considered asking Paulette to go along this morning, so the guys could see the kind of nice, sweet girl they'd be helping to avenge, but thought better of it. He felt he could just as easily make his case to them that they'd simply be along for protection, sort of like a backup if needed.

After showering and getting dressed, he went to the garage and connected the Jeep Cherokee's battery to his charger to at least get it started and went back in the house and waited twenty minutes to make sure the charge held. He told Johnny his objective and said he'd stay in touch and they made plans to meet up after lunch.

Johnny returned to the kitchen, where Betty, happy to have an audience, was regaling her new friend with her family history and local lore, such as the time she saw Nat "King" Cole sing at the nearby Westchester County Center, "not long before he passed," and danced to Ray Charles's eight-piece band on another occasion at the same venue. Or the time, she and her underage girlfriends went to see Ike & Tina Turner at the Ham House, a bucket of blood next to the railroad tracks, and a fight broke out, ending in a stabbing and Ike bashing the stabber over the head with a solid body Fender Stratocaster guitar.

"But I was just a girl, about your age, honey, and that was before I met my husband and became a church woman," she laughed at the memory. Seeing Johnny in the doorway, she said, "Now don't you dare tell Pete. He likes to think I was always Mother Teresa."

"*Omerta*, Betty. That's what we Italians call it. It means silence. Your secret is safe with me."

"Oh, I know a little Italian, baby. You forget, Greenburgh is half Italian and half colored. You think I don't know that my son is probably halfway over to Varvaro's, that little store on the corner of Russell Street where that Babe Telesco and Patsy Pelligrino stay?"

"Can't put nothing over on you, eh, Bett?"

"You better know it, boy. Now where you two off to this morning?"

"It's such a beautiful day. I thought we might take a ride up to the dam. You wanna come along?"

"No, I need to watch my story. I gotta keep up with Victor and Nikki on *The Young and the Restless*. The story's gettin' hot now. Nikki's fixin' to throw him out the house and that darn Phyllis has set her sights on poor, dumb Nick yet again."

"Wait, how many times has she done that in the past forty years?"

"I lost count twenty years ago," the two of them laughed, "but when you're hooked your hooked, and you don't dare miss a chapter."

"Well you let me know what happens, okay?"

He and Paulette showered, dressed and got into the white BMW, and headed north, up Hillside Avenue toward the Kensico reservoir.

As his mother predicted, Pete pulled up in front of Varvaro's and went inside. Ninety-one year old Antoinette Telesco, one of the seven Varvaro sisters, widow of Pep Telesco and mother of Babe and Gyp, three of the roughest characters in White Plains underworld history, sat on a padded wooden chair in front of the counter, smoking a pipe. The late Pep, an independent soul who never joined a mob, once owned a twenty-five acre plot of land adjoining the village of Silver Lake in North White Plains where, even before the hippie era, he grew marijuana to sell to those locals who enjoyed a taste of the weed. This had been a lucrative part of the family business as far back as his grandfather, who sold what was then called "reefer" in the 1930s when one who imbibed was called a viper.

"Hey Pete! How the hell are you? How long you in town for this time?"

"Hard to say, Miss Antoinette. Concerts have been cancelled all over the country, so I'm in between engagements."

"Why don't you go up to Metropolis and make a couple-a loops?"

They shared a laugh and he said, "I'd be lucky if I could do eighteen holes at my age, much less thirty-six. You seen Babe and them this morning?"

"He should be around here soon. Probably just woke up, with his lazy ass. What you want with him? You need him to hurt somebody or somethin'?"

"Maybe. Or maybe just to have my back on this thing I need to do later on. I need to see who's around who might want to take a ride with me over to Port Chester tonight or in the next night or so."

Her family background told her it was best not to ask for details. "Leave me your number and I'll let him know you was looking for him."

Like New Orleans, blue collar White Plains was a unique mix of black and southern Italian inhabitants and, as in New Orleans, local Italian speech patterns reflected elements of both dialects. Having lived on Russell Street her entire life, Antoinette was a prime example of this phenomenon.

He wrote his cell number on her matchbook cover and climbed back in the Cherokee, then headed over to Battle Hill to see who might be on the corner. Once there, he spotted Donald Sledge from the Swans and Doc Robinson of the Master-tones in the vacant lot across the street, but it was too early to be singing, or too late, considering their advanced age. They were waiting for the liquor store to open so they could pick up a little morning taste, a little eye-opener.

It was a beautiful warm, sunny September day. Johnny navigated as Paulette drove the three miles up Hillside Avenue, past Mt. Calvary Cemetery and crossed the Bronx River Parkway, arriving at the beautiful, granite structure in nine minutes. He had her park on a service road off to the west side of the reservoir, so they could walk across. After the destruction of the World Trade Center in 2001, and the subsequent fears of further terrorist attacks, the roadway across the dam had been closed off, but in 2012 it was reopened, but only to pedestrian and bicycle traffic.

Out on the water, they could see a few small boats with men fishing for the brown trout that were stocked each year by the Department of Environmental Conservation. There had been a shortage of rain that summer and the lake was down, enough so that he was able to point out an old church steeple rising almost to the water's level, where the once-upon-a-time hamlet of Kensico had been flooded to make room for the reservoir, when the original dam was built in the 1880s to provide water for New York City. When that was later found to be insufficient, the current dam was built between 1913-1917. Both were constructed by some fifteen hundred largely Southern Italian laborers, mainly stonemasons imported from the Old Country, many illegally. Hence, the derogatory term "wop," which meant "without papers."

The man who brought them over was named Santo "Sammy" Santoro, no known relation to Johnny or Nicky. He owned the entire three block length of Ferris Avenue, which contained a long row of less than desirable identical housing, where the immigrants were forced to live, next to the noise of the New York Central Railroad's Harlem Division tracks. They had to buy their overpriced provisions from a Santoro-owned store on the block and worshipped at the tiny Church of the Assumption, also on Ferris Avenue, as they were unwelcome at the nearby St. John's. Italians who'd graduated to the working class and higher, attended Our Lady of Mt. Carmel, on Orawaupum Street, a beautiful church with a 200-foot high campanile topped off by a gold-leaf dome.

In addition to the church steeple in the lake, Paulette thought she could see another building or two under the dark water, but on second thought, realized it may only have been her imagination. Behind them, on the opposite side of the roadway, they could look down upon the majestic stonework and the gargoyles that decorated the magnificent structure. For the fourth anniversary of 9/11, a memorial had been constructed in the plaza below and dedicated to the one hundred and nine Westchester County residents who died in the Twin Towers that day. As they ambled back to the car, she held his hand, her fingers entwined with his.

His phone rang. It was Carole. She'd spoken to her boss, imploring him to see if it was possible to put Johnny on the fast track to an insurance settlement. Could he come by the office this morning before lunch? He eagerly agreed and they took off.

Within the half hour, after identifying themselves to the guard downstairs and being admitted to the building, they were stepping off the elevator at the top floor, where a receptionist escorted them down the long, tiled hallway toward Carole's office. On their right was a floor-to-ceiling window that ran the length of the four-story building with a view of the traffic flowing on Interstate 287. To their left, on a level below, were numerous cubicles where workers typed away on their PCs, trying in vain to keep up with the many claims submitted in the wake of the attacks.

Near the end of the hallway, beneath their feet was, instead of the floor tiles, soft, expensive carpeting for another thirty feet until they reached a door with a small sign that read "Carole Holman, executive assistant" and were welcomed by their friend.

"Mr. Griffin's anxious to meet you. He's a big music fan and even has some of the albums you played on."

Over his years in the business, Johnny had become used to this kind of recognition and, under the circumstances, was relieved to have found a fan.

Griffin, a husky, balding man in his early 50s who looked as if he'd once played football in school, extended his hand and said, "I can't tell you what an honor it is to meet you Mr. Santoro. I'm a big fan and play a little myself." He talked a bit about his high school garage band, what kind of guitar and amp he owned and how a few of his now-middle aged friends get together one night a week to play music, an admission not unfamiliar to Johnny.

"Carole's given me all your information and it looks like we should be able to put you on the fast track to being made whole. It helps to have friends like Carole and fans like me in your corner. I know nothing can make up for all the memories you've lost, but the least we can do for you is to make sure you have the financial wherewithal to start over."

"You're very kind, Mr. Griffin. I didn't know what I was going to do."

"This is what we do, Johnny. When I get the chance to do it for someone I admire, it means even more to me. Is this your daughter Stacy? I saw her name in your files and didn't realize she was so young."

"No sir. I apologize for not introducing her. Mr. Griffin, this is my friend, Paulette de Saint Marie. Paulette, this is Mr. Griffin."

"Any relation to Jacques?"

"Why yes," said Paulette, "He's my father."

"Why didn't you tell me, Carole? See this ring, Paulette?" He lifted his hand to reveal a Freemason's ring on his finger. "Does it mean anything to you?" Griffin paused for effect, and then, "Johnny, between Carole's family connection and your friendship with Paulette, I'm 99.9% sure I can have your money for you by tomorrow, the next day at the latest. If you need a reference or a proper introduction to a local bank, we'd be happy to provide it, although I'm sure Mr. de Saint Marie can take care of you in that area."

Hands were shaken and thanks were proffered, and Carole walked Johnny and Paulette to the elevator. "Mr. Griffin's as good as his word, so you're covered. I got this job twenty years ago with him, thanks to my aunt's Eastern Star ring, and I've been his right-hand gal ever since. There's a world of loyalty in that ring. Paulette, you be sure and tell your dad what you saw here today, okay? Will I see you all at the house tonight?"

"I'm not sure, Carole. Your brother and I may have something important to do, and we won't know until later. But I'll see you tomorrow, for sure."

CHAPTER 19

HANDSOME TONY CALABRESE'S FACE, WITH HIS square jaw and those rows of shiny white teeth, was now being seen on every news channel in the country, with all the glowing publicity engendered by the capture of the grid hacker. His opinions were sought on every subject, from his favorite Italian places to eat to the name of his tailor to who he thought was going to win the World Series, with a little politics thrown in for good measure. Very little, because he took great pains to avoid any controversy at all times, knowing the best route to political success was to appear to be all things to all people. His mentor, Nicky Santoro, had schooled him well.

Some pundits were even beginning to speak of him as a potential candidate for president in the upcoming special election. But Nicky, who'd spent a lifetime taking the pulse of the American public, had other ideas.

"Man, don't you see? This country still ain't ready for no guinea president. Giuliani was a good man, but they passed on him, remember? They afraid of us. Never lose sight of that."

"But I'm hot right now, Nicky. I gotta grab the moment."

"No, you don't gotta grab no fucking moment. I'm workin' on something, so hold your horses and don't go gettin' *la gran' testa*, the big head."

"What you mean, Nicky? I gotta do *something*."

"Listen to me. You will be president, I promise you, but when the time is right. Remember, we made Kennedy president," he reminded him. "And you know how that shit turned out. Them double-crossing Kennedys was a bad bunch, from the daddy on down to that fat-ass whoremonger Teddy. Right now, the stupid Republicans ain't got a chance. They hitched their mule to Trump last time out. Now even the ones who had a shot before don't no more. They're fucked. *Nel culo*, up the ass. The Democrats know how to play that bullshit celebrity game better than anybody. They'll either run some asshole movie star or turn some nobody into a star, like they did Obama. They got that shit down pat."

"So how do we fight that?"

"The rubes are suckers for celebrity, so we just need to find us a bigger, more likeable one, and run him as an independent, with you as VP."

"You got somebody in mind?"

"The Rock. Dwayne mother fuckin' Johnson. Everybody loves the fucking Rock. World-wide, man! He's moderate, straight down the middle. And he's half-black like Obama, so he'll grab votes from all sides. And he's better looking than you, even. People are sick of both parties, an' how they always bad mouthin' each other. He comes off as sincere. I got a line on his people and I'm gonna be talkin' to them before the week is out. Don't worry, and if anything should happen to him, you next in line, so just be cool and wait your turn."

They disconnected their Skootch app and Tony was left with thoughts of his future, a big, beautiful future. He trusted Nicky's judgement, because Nicky knew, better than anyone, how the average Joe and Jane think, and, as Nicky always said, "There's more of them than there is the freaks on the fringes."

Next, Nicky checked in with Vito Gennaro, to see if everything was a go for the Port Chester situation.

"Looks good for tonight," reported Vito, "I got the Red Wings lined up and waiting on my word. I'll get back to you tomorrow and let you know how it went."

"No man, call me tonight, late as you want; I'm up late. Listen, I got something else going you gonna wanna be a part of. Can't tell you yet, but it's gonna be fucking big time. You gonna call Johnny or should I?"

"Yeah, I'll take care of it Nicky. Him and his friend are waiting to hear from me. I'm just gonna wait a little longer till I'm a hundred percent sure the Red Wings are all set to go."

Nicky's other phone rang. It was a woman from The Rock's organization. Now that Nicky knew Johnson's agents didn't mind talking to someone like him, the door was open to deeper discussion. He kept the conversation plain and simple. He wanted to secure his relationship with Jacques before delving any deeper with The Rock's people. He had to play this very carefully, keeping all the balls in the air at once, a skill at which he was a master.

CHAPTER 20

BY EVENING, PETE WAS FEELING A LOT BETTER about the coming engagement. He'd managed to round up Babe Telesco, as well as Dicey Williams, a fellow former Navy Seal, and Roosevelt "Stoney" McCrea, who'd been in Special Forces in the Middle East, training the Kurds in the ways of assassination. So, Pete now knew he and Johnny had experienced back-up they could trust implicitly.

The five of them, along with Tommy and Ray Annunziato, rode in Pete's Cherokee, Tommy's girth crowding his seatmates in the middle row, exiting Interstate 287 at Westchester Avenue and heading along back streets into the black section of town. Dicey was familiar with the area. His long-time girlfriend, D'Neese, lived not far from their destination and he knew all the best escape routes, a necessity for a White Plains guy dating a girl from Port Chester. Unlike big cities such as New York, where the street gangs that protected their own turf had names, the gangs of lower class Westchester and Connecticut identified with their particular towns.

It was still early, so they stopped off to kill time at Texas Lunch on Main Street, up from the Lifesaver factory, where Millie Garfield, a hard-edged woman in her late 50s who wore her short, gray hair in an Elvis "D.A.," or duck's ass, and always had a half-smoked cigarette dangling from her lower lip, made the best chili dogs on the planet.

As they downed their chili dogs, followed by corn muffins, to soak up the grease, they were in constant contact with the Red Wings, via cell phone. Both Tommy and Johnny had the numbers of the crew's leader, Jimmy "Gums" Pagano and his second-in-command, Paulie Vastola, on quick dial. That way, if either leader should lose contact, there was an alternate means of communication.

The snipers were in position on the adjoining rooftops. There were eyes in both the front and rear of the house, as well. No one was going to leave that house without being seen. The Red Wings were awaiting Tommy's signal, the blast from the grenade, which, upon receiving his text, Paulie would toss down the coal shoot.

Stomach muscles were tight, perspiration ran from armpits, hearts were pounding, adrenaline was pumping and all were on high alert, filled with the kind of apprehension that comes in a life or death situation.

In the basement, Tupac Prentiss nervously paced the cement floor, banging his fist against the metal side of the furnace, hyper from the cocaine he'd snorted earlier. He couldn't put his finger on it, but he had a bad feeling something just wasn't right. The paranoid instincts that were a large part of his sociopathic, psychological make-up had served him well over the years and tonight looked to be no exception.

Four of his guys were seated at a table, playing bid whist, a high-intensity card game, similar to bridge, that had been popular in the black community since the Civil War. It is a game of serious strategy and skill. One player tries to figure out what cards his opponent has, by way of card counting and assessing the body language of the person on the opposite side of the table. It is also a game of psychology in which "trash talking" is employed to throw the opponent off his or her game. It is played almost entirely by black men and women of every class, cultural and educational level, none of which is any predictor of whom the better player may be.

Cannabis dulled the senses of the card players and observers alike. Cheap wine of the screw-off cap variety was flowing and the voices were growing louder as the game became more intense with each hand dealt.

"You gonna play or what, man? You so slow you come in third in a two-man race."

"Fuck you, man, you so slow you gonna cross the finish line in a pine box."

"Mother fucker, I'll put your black ass in pine box, if you don't play your card."

"You ugly, bug-eyed mother fucker, I'll play my goddamn card when I'm good and ready."

"Ugly? Shit, *you* so ugly, you make onions cry."

"Yeah? You so ugly, your mama had to feed you with a slingshot."

"Don't be talkin' 'bout my mama. Your mama so dumb, when they say it chilly outside, she grab a bowl and a spoon."

"Your mama so fat, she crossed in front of the TV and I missed three episodes of my story."

The two stood up and just as fisticuffs were about to commence, the grenade slid from Paulie's hand, down the coal shoot and exploded next to the water heater, cracking it open and causing the scalding water to burn two of the gang and shards of sharp metal to embed in the flesh of three others.

As the boys ran toward the stairs, Tupac, safely sheltered by the furnace, paused to consider his options. More savvy than the others, he rightly presumed the explosion was a ploy to force the gang up and out of the house through the only stairwell. He decided to take the gamble of shimmying up the shoot and hope that no one would be waiting.

As some of the gang ran toward the front door, others made their way to the back, where they were met by crowbars and baseball bats to their knees and brought down hard. The same fate awaited those who exited the front of the building. The sounds of cracking femurs, tibiae and fibulae were covered only by the screams of their owners, as the Harlem Red Wings wreaked vengeance for the rape of Patricia de Saint Marie, without mercy upon the young thugs. These were followed by the dull thud of boots crushing ribs and stomping heads, as Tupac's crew lay on the ground in their own blood, tears and teeth.

Being highly trained in the military ways of battle, Pete was unused to the gang warfare employed by the Red Wings, but with no advance time to train them, he had decided to let them do things the way that worked for them in the past. But it was frustrating for him and his guys to go into this op without proper flack jackets and silent communication equipment. What if a cell phone rang, even on vibration, and gave away the location of one of his men?

"Let's hit the alley," Pete suggested, "This Prentiss kid ain't stupid. He'll try the coal shoot."

So, they ran around the side of the building, just in time to spot Tupac turning a corner past the house next door. The sniper on that roof was unable to get off a shot, as the kid stuck too close to the wall below. As Babe Telesco rounded the corner, he saw him turn up another alley across the street and gave chase, followed by Pete, calling directions on his phone.

By the time he and the others reached the house, Tupac was two-thirds the way up a fire escape and about to kick through a window on the top floor.

Pete shouted out orders, "Dicey, you and Stoney hit the back. Tommy, you and Ray go through the front, and Babe and I will take the fire escape. Johnny, you wait down here. He might be armed."

With only a small pistol from Pete's stockpile for protection, and only limited shooting experience, it was clear he'd be of little use in a firefight, so he waited.

Prentiss, in the apartment of one of his gang members, went to where he knew a gun was kept and grabbed it, along with a fistful of ammunition, while he considered the safest means of escape. Well aware that his very

life depended on his next move and, knowing this was the most important decision he would ever have to make, he chose to go up, to the roof.
A good running start, and a lucky jump, could take him to the roof next
door and then perhaps to another, where a girl he knew lived and might
allow him inside.

Guns drawn, Ray entered the front and Dicey came in the back and
they went up the stairs while Tommy and Stoney remained at their respective doorways in case Tupac managed to elude the other two and come
down. Pete and Babe entered the apartment through the broken window
and, finding it empty, headed out the door, shouting below.

"Anybody seen him?"

"The fucking little fuck ain't down here," Tommy yelled, so Pete and
Babe went up to the roof, in time to see Prentiss leaping to the roof next
door. The sniper took a shot but missed when Tupac zigged. By then the
kid was on the third roof and out of range.

Pete saw him enter the door on the third roof and phoned Tommy to
let him know which building he was in. Everybody ran to their respective
entrances at that house and took the same positions as at the first.

This was not the type of neighborhood from which many residents
were likely to call the police at the sound of gunshots or cries of pain. People
here knew it was safer to mind their own business. So, there would be no
sounds of sirens approaching.

Pete and Babe made the leaps, from one rooftop to the next, and then
the third, where they'd seen Prentiss enter the doorway. Pete opened the
door and they stepped aside, and when there was no gunshot, they entered
and quietly slipped down the stairs to the third floor and listened at the first
door they came to. Hearing no sound from within, he tapped the barrel of
his gun against the wood and held one hand over the peephole.

The voice of a young woman said, "Who is it?" And Pete lied, "Open
up, police," and she did.

"Anyone in there?"

"No officer, just me," and they pushed their way inside. Finding the apartment empty, they turned to leave.

Prentiss, hearing the heavy footsteps above, saw his chance and quietly slipped out of the apartment, where he was hiding directly below, and moved toward the stairs from the second floor down to the first, where he assumed the enemy awaited him in the dark and so, pointed his weapon straight ahead in a crouch. Pressing his tiny body to the wall, he made his way down the front stairs, one by one, to where Tommy Annunziato lay in wait, lit from behind by a streetlight outside and a twenty-five watt bulb down the hall.

At almost 300 pounds, Annunziato made for a large target. Suddenly, only a few feet apart in the semi-dark, the two saw each other at the same moment and both fired. Tommy missed and Tupac's bullet tore through the fat man's left arm but failed to knock him down. In a flash, astoundingly quick for a man his size, he took one step forward. His right hand moved rapidly and his curled index finger struck its target. A split second later, Prentiss's eyeball lay on the hallway floor and blood gushed through the fingers of his hand, as he pressed it to his face, screaming in pain.

Tommy's brother Ray emerged from the apartment he'd been searching at that moment and, as Pete and Babe looked down from the steps above, he put three slugs into the body of the little rapist. Pete phoned Johnny to come and see, so he could confirm to Nicky Santoro that Paulette's mother had been avenged. He arrived just in time to see Tupac Prentiss foul his pants and take his final breath.

Although growing up the nephew of the head of the New Orleans Mafia, and though his best friend Pete, a former Navy Seal, was schooled in the art of assassination and who had on occasion been forced to kill during the Iraq war, Johnny was not a man of violence. What he saw there on the floor by the stairs sickened him.

The eyeless socket in Tupac's twisted face, his eyeball lying on the filthy linoleum, the blood oozing from the three rounds Ray had put into his little torso, and it was all he could do to keep his chili dogs down in that hallway.

He knew all too well what men like the Red Wings were capable of: the brutality, the fracturing of bones, the stomping on faces, ribs and testicles, such as they had done to other bangers from other gangs in the name of street justice. However justified, murder had been committed and, if they were discovered, the law would certainly have something to say about it.

Pete and his friends, having served their country in battle, in kill-or-be-killed situations, knew what it felt like to take a life. To hesitate, for even one split-second, could mean the difference between walking away alive to fight again or remaining on the battlefield, a bloody corpse to be bagged and flown home in a box, covered by a red, white and blue flag and spoken over by some phony politician who had to read your name off a sheet of paper, to be forgotten five minutes later, leaving your parents and loved ones to ache for the remainder of their days.

This had been no kill-or-be-killed situation. It was a carefully planned out revenge killing. Everyone involved would feel differently later about what they'd done. There would be different degrees of rue, regret, remorse or even a twinge of guilt, such as what Johnny was already beginning to feel throughout his body.

Rationalize all you want, he thought, *tonight you were a part of something wrong, something really bad, and, someday, somehow, you're going to have to pay for your part in this.*

He came out of this reverie as Dicey and Stoney applied a tourniquet to Tommy's injury and determined that the bullet had passed through the layers of fat in his arm. Both battle-tested men were well versed in the art of first aid. They got some hydrogen peroxide and clean towels from the nearest apartment and pronounced him well enough to make it to an East Harlem doctor who could always be counted on to never report the bullet wounds of Vito's crew to the police or anyone else.

The little group made their way back to the pre-arranged meeting spot where they found the Red Wings waiting. All were safe and accounted for. But the occasion was too somber for high fives or fist bumps. The sound of sirens in the distance told them it was time to split up and head for their various home bases.

As the Jeep Cherokee made its way back to Greenburgh, Johnny texted Nicky and Vito: *Batter struck out. Game over.*

CHAPTER 21

AFTER EVERYONE WAS DROPPED OFF, THEY DROVE to Pete's house, where Paulette was anxiously waiting with Betty and Carole. Only she knew where they'd been and what they'd been doing. Dinah Washington was singing "Where Are You" on the stereo, as they walked in the door.

They did their best to put on happy faces, but Carole suspected something wasn't right and now realized her perception about Paulette's uneasiness over the course of the evening had been correct. As for Betty, she was just happy to see her boy's face.

Paulette ran to them and threw her arms around both men.

"I'm so happy you're all right," she said, and Johnny gave her a look that said, "Be cool," and she got the hint. In an attempt to cover her mistake, she said, as nonchalantly as she knew how, "The newsfeed on my phone said there'd been a terrible four car accident on the Bronx River Parkway. One of the vehicles was a Jeep Cherokee and I was afraid it might be you guys."

Carole sucked her teeth at the blatant lie but said nothing. Pete gave her a quick sideways glance, then looked away. Betty said, "Anybody want some of this peach pie? It's the end of the season, but they're still very sweet."

Johnny sat up and said, "Heck yeah! I'd love me some peach pie, Bett! Cut me a nice big slice." The mood in the room improved, as Dinah swung out with "Destination Moon," and all sat down for some dessert. "How

about a little ice cream to go with that? I got Haagen-Dazs vanilla or cookies and cream," said Betty, smiling brightly.

The remainder of the evening continued in this vein, surface pleasantry
with a sinister undercurrent, apparent to everyone except Pete Holman's
mother, who remained clueless. Wishing to savor every moment she could
with her boy, she stayed up well past her usual bedtime. But in the end,
she had to beg off and hit the hay, before long falling to sleep with the late
local Channel 4 news on the TV in her bedroom.

"In other news, up in Port Chester tonight, gang violence erupted with
some twenty gang members viciously beaten within an inch of their lives
and one shooting death. The injured were transported to local hospitals.
Police say they have no clues as to who the assailants might be. The name
of the deceased is being withheld until next of kin can be notified. And
now, in other news..."

With Betty off to dreamland, Carole finally spoke. "Okay, you three.
Out with it. What's going on here? Where have you two boys been? And
don't tell me 'nothing,' you hear?"

After an uncomfortable silence that felt like an eternity, Pete spoke.
"Carole, there are some things that it's best for as few people to know
about as possible, and this night is one of those times. That's all I'm going
to tell you. I love you, but you need to accept what I'm saying, and never
ask me again."

"Sounds serious. Johnny? You're not going to help me out here?"

Johnny shook his head and Paulette looked down. She didn't know the
gruesome details, and perhaps never would, but she knew that, whatever
had transpired, it was extremely serious.

"Okay, but don't expect me to tell you I like it," said Carole. "But I
understand, so I won't ask again."

Something serious indeed had occurred. On the news in the morning,
it would be ascribed to that all-purpose euphemism, "gang violence," and

promptly forgotten about, just another example of the brutality of the kind of people no one cares about anyway.

There had been at least one murder, however justified, and maybe more when the injuries were added up. The Red Wings too, had done a lot of damage in those few moments of virtually one-sided mayhem. At the very least, those gang bangers could count on weeks, maybe months, in traction, at White Plains Hospital. Whether all of them would survive was a question no one could answer at this point.

The question on Johnny's mind was, how much to tell Paulette? She needed to know, as did her parents, that the ones who'd perpetrated those vicious acts upon Patricia had been punished, and that the punishment had been at least equal to the crime. But finding the right words to describe it to a gentle, nineteen-year old girl was going to be difficult.

Carole eventually went off to bed, leaving the others to stay up and talk. It was left to Johnny to fill Paulette in. "Let me just say this. Your mom has been avenged and she never has to worry about any blowback from those animals. I know a part of you wants to know more, but it's best you don't. Can you deal with that?"

She held him in her arms and said, "Yes, I can. I was so worried for your safety, Johnny. I don't know what I'd do if anything were to happen to you. I've never lost anyone I loved before."

Johnny and Pete exchanged looks.

He was struck dumb by her words, namely the "L word," something he never expected to ever hear again at his age from any woman, much less one so young and beautiful. He didn't know what to make of it. Her generation tended to be hyperbolic in their free use of the phrase *I love you*, and the self-protective part of him wanted to write it off as nothing more than that. *But what if*, he asked himself. *What if she really means it? What do I do with that? What do I do with her? What can I possibly offer a girl like that?*

He allowed himself a selfish thought. His own father's second marriage after his mother died had been to a woman fifteen years younger, and a nurse at that. She took care of him in his final years, even into senility, and long after his passing, she carried a great love for him within her soul, never taking another man to her bed or to her heart until her own passing, more than a decade later. She was a woman of the old ways. And the old ways dictated that a woman loves once, and forever.

Yet, this was no mere fifteen years' difference. Johnny was old enough to be father to her parents, old enough to be her grandfather. He'd known girls with "daddy complexes" before. Girls like that abound in the rock'n'roll world, but this was ridiculous, he thought. Was it fair of him to steal her prime years? On the other hand, what about what *she* wanted? Wasn't that something to be taken into consideration as well?

In the end, despite his moral quandary, he decided to leave it alone, at least until if and when she brought it up again. Hell, it may have been nothing more than a slip of the tongue in an emotional moment of relief that her two friends had made it safely back from a dangerous mission. He was a procrastinator from way back, and if ever there was a time when procrastination was called for...

He decided to wait until at least tomorrow, after her family had been told the fate of one Tupac Prentiss and his sorry-ass friends.

CHAPTER 22

THE NEXT EVENING, TOMMY, RAY AND THE members of the Red Wings who had participated in the one-sided Battle of Port Chester were treated to dinner in the back room of Patsy's, which Vito had set aside for the celebration. Each man was handed an envelope with his name on it, filled with cash.

The tables were overflowing with delicious Sicilian favorites: *Arancini*, stuffed rice balls coated with breadcrumbs and fried in olive oil; *Crocche*, a concoction of mashed potato and egg, also fried and covered in bread-crumbs; *Maccu*, a Sicilian soup prepared with dried, crushed fava beans and fennel; *Caponata*, an eggplant stew; *Sarde a Beccafico*, sardine rolls with raisins and pine nuts; *Pesce spade*, or stuffed swordfish rolls; *Pasta alla Norma*; Sicilian orange salad; *Pasta con le sarde*, a pasta cooked with sardines and, as a special treat, Vito's wife Cecile sent along her famous *braciole*, miniature ones that were so tasty that women had been said to achieve orgasm after only one bite.

The *salsiccia* were made in the tenement basement of Vincent Di Lugo of 116th Street, directly across from Our Lady of Mt. Carmel church. The large meatballs were made of pork, beef and veal with just the right amount of bread crumbs and slow-cooked all day in a pot of marinara sauce, where they were joined by pork chops and pulled beef, simmering until the meat fell off the bones. Two jaw bones were procured, one cow and one hog, cooked for eight hours until tender and served with nothing more than the perfect amount of garlic, lemon and salt.

After dinner, the long table was loaded down with a vast array of desserts: *biscotti Regina*; *Gelo di melone*, a watermelon pudding; *Cassata Siciliana*, a sponge cake in liqueur, layered with slices of sweetened ricotta mixed with candied fruit and chocolate bits, covered with an icing made from sugar and egg whites; *Bacione di Taormina* or Taormina Kiss, a cocoa and almond filling, covered with a pistachio coating; also, your more commonplace *Marzipan* and *cannoli*.

Enormous quantities of grappa and homemade red wine, made by the last great East Harlem wine maker in his basement on Second Avenue near 121st Street were consumed as the men's conversations ran from the previous night's victory to conquests past, and enemies and friends long departed from this earth. Everyone was in good spirits and staggered home, stuffed to their ears.

The fare at *Maison* de Saint Marie that evening was decidedly less exotic, and much less calorie laden. A simple, all-American meal of pot roast with mashed potatoes, carrots and green peas, along with a simple salad of iceberg lettuce, tomatoes and croutons, and Paulette's favorite, angel food cake covered in strawberries for dessert. She preferred frozen to fresh, for the sweet, tasty red juice. Michelle came down from her room to join the family at dinner, her eyes on emails and texts from her friends the whole time, then returning upstairs when she was finished eating. She was well behaved, which was always a plus in any fourteen-year old girl.

After dinner, the others adjourned to the library, where Johnny had the unpleasant task of reporting the previous night's events. Sparing the women the bloodier parts, he managed to convey the fact of Tupac Prentiss's death without turning Patricia's stomach with details. The family was relieved to learn that there was no danger of reprisal, as the young gangsters had been given no reason for the attack. They had plenty of enemies. It was unknown who or how many other homes they had vandalized that fateful night, so there was no way the beatings could ever be tied to the family.

Tearfully, Patricia thanked Johnny and Pete profusely for avenging her and making her feel safe again in her own home, and then excused herself and her daughter, so her husband could speak with the two men alone.

"When you're done with your man talk, Johnny," said Paulette as she was leaving, "please knock on my door, okay?"

Johnny nodded and she pulled the sliding doors together behind her.

"I want to say something," Jacques began, "You and your friends have done what I wished I'd been man enough to do, and I'd like to thank you from the bottom of my heart. My family and I will always be indebted to you both. You can consider me a friend, in every way that matters."

He took a sip of his digestif, a *pousse-café*. It was his favorite, Veuve J. Goudoulin 1980 Vieuxe Bas Armagnac. He loved the beautiful color with its green highlights, and the nutty, licorice taste. As it went down, he thought of how much he preferred it to cognac for its more robust flavor.

"Johnny, can we speak freely here, or do you and I need to be alone," he said, indicating Pete.

"You can say anything in front of Pete, as long as he feels comfortable. He's my soul brother and I trust him more than anyone I know."

"Very well. Your uncle has hinted of some plans in the offing that are of great interest to me and to my colleagues, both here and abroad. I'd like to know the best way to open up further conversation on these matters at the earliest date that is convenient for all concerned. I understand that your uncle is not a young man so I am more than willing to travel to New Orleans if that would be easier for him."

"My uncle doesn't like to leave home. He never has, so if you don't mind, I'm sure you'd love the city. I can arrange a meeting and guarantee all the privacy you'd ever want. You want me to call him now?"

"If you don't mind, yes, please. The white phone on the desk is a secure, encrypted line. Privacy is often necessary in my business too."

Johnny dialed Nicky's secure number. The old man picked up and Johnny filled him in on the conversation in the New Orleans Sicilian dialect only they could understand and asked if he'd rather continue via Skootch.

"No, we safe enough on these lines. Put him on," he replied in English.

The discussion was brief, just a few basics. They agreed that Jacques would fly down two days hence. After they hung up, Jacques phoned his pilot and instructed him to ready the company jet for flight from Westchester County Airport the morning after next.

Pete asked if he'd be needed on the trip and when told not, he opted to stay home to spend time with his mother and sister and to catch up with old friends. Johnny told Jacques how much Paulette had enjoyed her time in Metairie and suggested they ask if she'd like to go along. His business prevented him from spending as much time with his daughter as he'd wish, so he thought this was a good idea and suggested Johnny be the one to inform her that she was welcome to join them.

Pete took his leave and headed across county to the house on Oak Street, while the two men ascended the stairway, Jacques toward his wife's room and Johnny to Paulette's. As they stood in the hallway, Jacques started to speak on a subject he found uncomfortable. "My daughter is very fond of you, Johnny, and my family and I are forever grateful for all you've done." He hesitated. "I must be honest here, and I need to say that I am flummoxed by the age difference between you, as she seems to be growing closer to you. Paulette has a highly moral core, and I sense that you live by a certain code yourself. But I can't honestly say that I'm exactly comfortable with this. There are so many factors one could argue against such a relationship. Yet, I feel I...uh..." but not knowing what more to say, he stood uneasily for a moment and then, simply stretched out his hand to his new friend and, turning, he said, "Her happiness is all that matters," then entered Patricia's room.

When Johnny informed Paulette that she was invited to go with them to Nicky's, she hugged him and asked, "Was it your idea?" and he nodded.

"I knew it was you! I just knew it! Do you know how much I adore you?" She kissed him long and hard, her arms locking him in an embrace.

Again, he had that feeling, wondering if he was getting himself into something deeper than either of them could handle. But, as her kiss grew more passionate, he became aroused. Feeling his arousal, she pushed him backward onto her bed and undid the buttons on his shirt and jeans.

"You're staying the night, aren't you?" He was beyond resisting her or even wanting to do so. He lay there on his back, his pants and shorts down around his ankles, while she got up and turned off the light.

CHAPTER 23

GENERAL COLLEEN MCQUARTER WAS STILL THE face of authority on the nation's airwaves. Her serious, somber demeanor lent the impression that all was under control whenever she appeared on television to deliver the latest update. These were aired a minimum of three times daily, during newscasts or as "breaking news." As food and water once again began to fill the shelves of supermarkets and *bodegas* throughout the Northeastern sector, Americans were slowly learning to become themselves once again.

Heavily armed soldiers and Marines, along with the National Guard, still patrolled the streets, attempting to be as unobtrusive as possible, for men and women dressed in khaki and carrying assault weapons. Their orders were to be friendly and helpful, and to smile often at passersby. For the most part, citizens responded in kind.

But the Joint Chiefs understood that a strong military presence could only go so far before cries of "Fascist state" would be heard from some corners. Americans preferred their leaders in civilian garb. Thus, it had been decided that a special election would take place, so voters could pick a new president. And as they had in 1960, Nicky Santoro and his friends around the country considered it in their best interests to see to it that the next person to sit at the big desk in the Oval Office would be one of their own choosing.

To that end, he sent two of his men to Louis Armstrong New Orleans International Airport in one of the armored Cadillac Escalades he kept on the premises, to meet the company jet carrying Jacques de Saint Marie, along with Johnny and Paulette in tow. Rather than use the quicker Interstate 10 for the return trip each airport pick-up, the cautious driver generally liked to switch things up, taking different routes to confuse any possible tail. For this day's pick-up, he took Airport Road from Kenner to the compound in Metairie and, less than twenty minutes later, they pulled in past the heavy iron gate.

After a light lunch prepared by Carmine of garlic shrimp parmesan with pasta, a chopped salad and freshly baked Italian bread, Nicky sent Paulette down to the stables with a guard and instructions to have Antoine take her riding on the Palomino she'd befriended last time she was there. The horse was overjoyed to see her and showed his pleasure by rubbing his head against her body. She stroked his long nose and fed him an apple, then climbed aboard, bareback as before, and the three of them took off along the winding trails. She gave him his head, urging him to a fast gallop, so she could feel the fresh air on her face after being cooped up in the plane. The groom had no trouble keeping up, unlike the less experienced guard, whose bulk and unease in the saddle were more than apparent to his horse, who knew enough to trot along behind at a slower pace, so his rider wouldn't fall off.

Back at the house, Nicky, Jacques and Johnny were met by Tony Calabrese, who'd come from a lunch meeting in the 6th Ward at the refurbished, famed Dooky Chase. Whenever Tony came to the compound, Carmela Mancuso would somehow find an excuse to be close to the handsome U.S. senator, if only in the shadows of a dark corner. Like every woman in Louisiana past the age of menopause, her crush on the senator could not be denied. Politician that he was, he never failed to flash his best vote-getting smile, the one that made her old heart quiver and her eyes practically glaze over as her fantasies ran to thoughts of many crushes past.

"Can I get you anything, Mister Senator?"

"No thank you, Carmela, I'm just fine. How you doin' babe? Ain't seen you in too long. Everything okay which you?"

He patted her on the shoulder and she thought she might faint right there on the spot while Nicky shook his head at this nonsense. Her knees almost gave out from the excitement, as she somehow made it out of the room without peeing herself, while Jacques looked on in wonder at this elected official's effortless effect on the ancient woman, as she exited, humming a few bars of the old Fats Domino tune about finding one's thrill on Blueberry Hill.

The restaurant from which Tony had just come had long been a place for local and national black community leaders to hold meetings and strategy sessions since long before the Civil Rights Era. Dooky's widow, Leah, a celebrity in her own right and closing in on 100 years of age, still came in most days, as much for the value of her star power as for any need to manage the place. The senator loved her shrimp gumbo and bread pudding and when she knew in advance he was coming, made a special batch herself, just for him. Several paintings and sculptures from her personal collection of works by black artists like Jacob Lawrence and Elizabeth Catlett now resided on the walls of his home, gifts from an old black woman to her senator.

Tony, who was well regarded in the community, had regular lunches with these leaders at the venerable eating establishment to keep up his contacts and good will. Consequently, he could always count on the black vote at election time. From the onset of his political career, he'd been coached by Nicky regarding the value of "community relations" and could often be spotted strolling the streets of the 9th Ward, chatting up anyone from shop owners to laborers to the pimps and whores on the corner, with that big smile and a coin or two for the children who crowded around him, pulling at his coat and pant legs.

Now, in the lead-lined, windowless, sound-proofed room at Nicky Santoro's home, a meeting of far greater consequence was about to commence.

"Mr. Santoro," Jacques began, "first of all, allow me to express face-to-face my gratitude for what you and your friends did for my family. I can never repay you for your act of friendship."

"Jacques, there ain't nothing a man won't do for a friend, and now you have seen for yourself, Nicky Santoro is a good man to have for a friend." He paused, to let the implications of his statement settle in. "This man you see here, Tony Calabrese, can tell you just how good a friend I can be. His daddy worked on the docks as a screwman, packin' big bales of cotton into the holds of the ships. He was a union man to the core and you know what they did?"

"No, I'm unfamiliar with the history of your city's waterfront."

"The owners was trying to work these men half to death, keepin' wages down by bringing in colored boys who'd work cheaper. That's where people like my daddy came in, the Black Hand, Sicilians smart enough to figure out deals could be done, if the union was a real union, one that stuck together. The owners did what they always do; they tried to split the workers apart, black an' white. But people like my daddy and uncle Carlos, and Tony's daddy, they figured if black and white got together, they could rule the waterfront, and make more money for everybody in the process. And that's just what they did. You see what I'm getting' at?"

"I think I do. Please, continue."

"Think of it like if one of us is the whites and the other is the blacks. You know this country been messed up for a long time. Every day, people come to me. They say, 'Nicky, America was a whole lot better off when you all was running things back in the day,' and I think about that, and I can see they right. There was order. A man's word was good as gold. People knew where they stood, and what to expect."

"There's something to be said for that, yes. A certain order, yes?" Jacques now saw where this was heading.

"You damn right there is. Now your people, they been here in America since day one. How many of the Founding Fathers was Masons? A whole bunch, George Washington, old Ben Franklin, at least eight of 'em signed the Declaration of Independence. Your Freemasons even came up with the ideas and notions that built the greatest country in the history of the world. Then Roosevelt and his crowd tried to fuck it up and give it all away to Stalin and them god damn Russians."

As his anger grew, his language turned coarser.

"Them commies infiltrated our unions, then our schools and newspapers, until our chirren don't know nothing about how the world works no more. It's up to us to lead 'em in the right direction. Think about it, Jacques. The Freemasons and us, an unbeatable combination."

He let that thought settle for a moment. Tony was always impressed and a bit surprised at Nicky's knowledge of history. Many people over the decades who'd made the mistake of thinking his lack of familiarity with the niceties of proper English grammar was a sign of ignorance often woke up one day, only to find themselves out-smarted and their bank account a whole lot lighter.

"Nicky," said Jacques, "I do believe you may have come up with a solution for these troubled times in which we find ourselves."

"I know I have. In the old days, we could make a man a mayor, a governor or even president of the United States. But it's hard now. They got the TV, the movies, the news. They got the chirren brainwashed, from kindergarten to college. They got every dumb-ass movie star and rock'n'roll singer thinking they know something. And the stupid public listens to these assholes. Roy Rogers and Jimmy Cagney, Johnny Carson, they ain't never had no opinions. I can't even believe people can be so goddamn dumb. Their stupidity used to work for us, but now it works against us."

Tony chimed in here, "You fucking A right, Nicky!"

"You see? Tony knows what's what. Even though he's a *Calabrese*. His name ain't even Calabrese, you know. We changed it 'cause his real one was too long and hard for white people to say. You know what they say about people from Calabria? They *capo dost*, they got the hard head."

He tapped the side of his skull with his arthritic knuckles to illustrate and went on.

"It cost a billion dollars to create a president today, even more. But some things is worth the price you pay. Somebody's gonna pay it and it might as well be us. Now this man right here, Antonino Calabrese, is the best, most natural born politician I ever seen. An' I seen a shit load. The mother fucking best, you hear me? I know I can make him president. I got a plan. I just need the money to do it right. That's where you and your crowd comes in, Jacques."

Nicky was a master of pausing for effect. He let that sentence sit there and linger a long, dramatic moment.

"Right now, you asking yourself, 'What's in it for me,' ain't you?"

Jacques smiled.

"What's in it for you is the same thing that's in it for me. We own the fucking leader of the so-called free world, man, and that ain't no small potatoes. That billion dollars will end up bein' a drop in the bucket. The way I see it, ain't nothing wrong with doin' some good and getting' paid for it at the same time."

His heart pounding now, Jacques completed the thought in his head. He understood that the combined interests of the Freemasons and the Mafia could be unstoppable and, in some weird way, perhaps even be best for the country and the world itself. He finally spoke, "And this time, unlike you and your friends' debacle with a certain Mr. Kennedy those many years ago, there will be no danger of the double cross."

"Now you got it. I raised this one from a pup. Taught him everything he knows. And he's in my pocket, ain't you, Tony?"

"No question, Nicky. We in this together, to our last breath."

"I couldn't of said it any better myself...to our last breath. You in, Jacques, or what?"

CHAPTER 24

SINCE IT WAS A FRIDAY, NICKY, WISHING TO cement his relationship with his new best bud, Jacques, suggested he stay the weekend and see the sights and "catch an earful of the greatest music in the universe." Paulette, a lover of music, pleaded with her dad and, unable to deny his beloved child anything she desired, it was decided they would put off leaving until Monday morning.

Nicky was not in the habit of going out in public often anymore, partially due to his advanced age, plus, he also thought it unwise, given his plans, for Tony to be seen in the company of a noted gangster. Why give the opposition ammunition if they didn't need to? So, the quartet of Jacques, Paulette, Johnny and Tony readied themselves for a night on the town in the Crescent City, courtesy of Nicky Santoro.

First stop was Liuzza's on Bienville, where the proprietor, Theresa Galbo, had the chef prepare a scrumptious family style meal. The table was interrupted throughout by a dozen or more glad handers, all wanting to kiss the ring of their senator. Tony greeted each one with that thousand-watt smile and a "Nice to see ya" that guaranteed one more vote come election time. The effect of his considerable charm did not go unnoticed by Jacques.

Then it was off to Tipitina's, the famed nightclub at the corner of Napoleon Avenue and Tchoupitoulas Street in the city's Uptown section.

The club was named in honor of the influential pianist, Henry Roeland "Roy" Byrd, better known as Professor Longhair, whose song, "Tipitina," was a New Orleans standard.

Starring onstage this night was Irma Thomas, known as the Soul Queen of New Orleans, best known for her 1960s recording of "Time Is On My Side," which became a best seller when covered by the Rolling Stones. She, like all too many New Orleans artists, never achieved the national fame her talent might have predicted. As the group was being seated, Irma was starting to sing "It's Raining," one of Johnny's favorites from her repertoire.

He turned to Paulette and pointed to the singer, "Listen to this song, it was written by Allen Toussaint. I call him the Cole Porter of New Orleans." A tear began to form in her eye when Irma sang the final line,

This is the time I'd love to be holding you tight, I guess I'll just go crazy tonight.

"Where do lines like that come from?"

"From heaven, baby," Johnny replied, "A line like that proves to me, there is a God." She took his hand in hers, as Irma repeated the last verse.

Spotting Johnny from the stage, one of the band members signaled him to come up and asked if he'd like to sit in. Irma spoke into the mic, "We have in our audience tonight a local boy made good, Mr. Johnny Santoro, who's played and recorded with everybody from Bonnie Raitt to Bobby 'Blue' Bland. Please, welcome him to the stage!"

As a sideman unused to such attention, he blushed and sauntered up. The guitar player handed him a black and white Silvertone electric of the kind sold at Sears at one time for thirty-five dollars. From the word *Shine* carved into the instrument's body, he recognized it as once having belonged to the late and legendary New Orleans musician and singer, Alvin "Shine" Robinson.

"What do you feel like doing, Johnny?" said Miss Thomas.

"How about Shine's big one, 'Something You Got?'"

They went into the funky masterpiece to the delight of everyone in the audience, who sang along with the chorus,

My, my, oh, oh, I love you so.

Johnny took a tasty solo in the middle to great applause, as he played recognizable licks from seemingly every Big Easy hit ever sung or played.

Smiling her beautiful smile as the song ended, Irma shouted into the mic, "We can't let him off with just one, can we?"

The crowd clapped, stomped their feet and shouted, "More! More!"

Not having touched a guitar since the night before the great tragedy that robbed him of his home and family, the music filled his soul with the joy that had been missing since that terrible morning and he said, "How about 'Don't Mess With My Man,' Irma?"

It was the first record she'd ever made, back when she was just another waitress, singing on the side with Tommy Ridgley's band. It had been only a mild hit nationally but was iconic in her hometown.

After a blistering eight-bar intro by Johnny, Irma blasted out the opening line, joined by every prostitute at the bar, and more than a few other women as well.

You can have my husband, but please don't mess with my man,
and brought down the house.

Irma walked off to a standing ovation, stepping back onto the small stage for another bow and a wave, but declining to do an encore. Energized by the moment, the band, wanting to keep playing, went into "Cissy Strut," the old Meters' song, and had people dancing on their chairs and tabletops. To the audience's delight, they played variations on the classic riff for some twenty minutes, before finally taking a break.

When he returned to their table, drenched in sweat, Jacques complimented him, saying, "Generally, my taste runs to Jacques Brel and Edith Piaf, but I can tell you are a master on your instrument. This music is new to me, but it truly speaks to something deep within these people, so much so that even I can feel it myself."

Tony popped up with, "By the time we get through with you, you ain't never gonna want to go home, my man. I can tell you fallin' in love with our fair city already."

It was nearly 2 am by the time Johnny texted the driver. The Cadillac Escalade pulled up to the front door of the club and the four of them climbed in. The driver dropped Tony off at his house and took the others back to the compound, where, still wide awake, they stayed up, seated around the kitchen table, talking about the fun they'd had to Nicky, who was also up at that late hour. He offered to make them some cold cut sandwiches but, still full from dinner, everyone begged off.

"How 'bout a little somethin' sweet? I got a couple *torrones* left over from supper," Nicky offered. When he pulled the nougat treats from the refrigerator, with the colorful slices of candied orange on top, none of them could resist. Just on the soft side of chewy, like taffy, the delicate, sweet flavor was just right for the end of a perfect evening.

CHAPTER 25

AS HE SETTLED INTO HIS BED, THE ONE HE'D
shared occasionally with his late wife for over sixty years, when she wasn't
sleeping in a room of her own, Nicky phoned Tony to get his take on how
the evening had gone.

"Oh man, these are great people. They lovin' our city after tonight."

"And more important," said Nicky, "They lovin' the shit out of you. I
want you to take 'em to the ball game tomorrow and show 'em another
good time."

"It oughta be a good game. They playing against Nashville."

The Nashville Sounds were the number one rivals of the New Orleans
Baby Cakes, the top Triple-A team in what was known by the unlikely
name, the Pacific Coast League. The two teams had once played for twenty-four innings straight in which the New Orleans crew, then known as the
Zephyrs, finally triumphed five to one. The battle was henceforth remembered as the "Music City Marathon." Then, in 2003, before the largest
crowd in the park's history, 11,925 paid, Nashville beat the Zephyrs, 1-0.
Tomorrow's game promised to be another good one.

The Baby Cakes' stadium, formerly known as Zephyr Field until 2016,
when it was renamed Shrine on Airline, was a 10,000-seat park in Jefferson
Parish, not far from Nicky's compound. Rumor had it that Carlos Marcello
had chosen the site because of its proximity to his home. Both he and Nicky

had air-conditioned luxury box suites, where they, their friends and business associates could watch from the window, on closed-circuit TV, or, for those who didn't mind the humidity or wanted to smoke, out on the balcony. Marcello's old suite, the most elaborate of the park's sixteen, now belonged to Nicky. It even had its own shower.

At breakfast, Nicky warned, "Now eat light, 'cause the food at the park is monstrous!"

Jacques asked if he might invite his pilot, Chuck, in return for keeping him apart from his family over the weekend, and his host gladly obliged and said he'd leave his name at the gate.

At noon they arrived and were accompanied by four stadium guards by elevator to the top floor, and to the suite. The names of Tony and Chuck were given to the two armed men who would be standing guard outside the locked door throughout the duration of the game.

The play-by-play man announced the presence of "Louisiana's own, our United States Senator, Handsome Tony Calabrese," to the cheers of the house. Tony stood on the balcony and gave the crowd his famous two-handed wave. Ladies of a certain age swooned when he revealed his pearly whites, which showed up brightly, like light bulbs on the Jumbotron.

"If anybody wants, there's a swimming pool and two hot tubs. We can run anybody outta there if you feel like takin' a little dip," said Nicky. "Just wait till you see the menu."

Paulette picked one up and noticed, in addition to the usual fare of fried catfish, muffulettas, po-boy sandwiches, jambalaya and pigskin nachos available to normal customers, the suites' guests were offered their choice of Oysters Rockefeller, Oysters Bienville, blackened redfish, dirty rice, crawfish *etouffee, pompano en papillote* or, that old stand-by, red beans and rice. The dessert menu included Bananas Foster, Doberge cake, pralines and, Johnny's favorite, beignets. She could feel her belly already expanding from all the good food she'd been eating since they arrived.

The game itself was a Battle Royale, fans of each team guzzling Coors beer throughout and spilling full cups of it from the upper level onto the heads of those below whose caps or shirts bore the wrong insignia. Sounds' fans had traveled *en masse* from Nashville to root their team on with all the volume their lungs could provide. By inning number five, fist fights were breaking out in the cheap seats, keeping security on their toes. These personnel were usually paid a bonus whenever the two bitter rivals met. Tempers were short, as the season was nearing its end and the two teams were vying for first place.

Things started off with a bang, when the Baby Cakes' star pitcher, veteran Scott Copeland gave up a home run off his first pitch. Nashville fans went wild, but Copeland calmed down and managed to strike out the next three batters in nine throws. The teams were evenly matched and the score remained 1-0 until the bottom of the ninth. There had been many "moments" and "almosts" with men left on base at the end of innings and disputed calls, resulting in items being tossed onto the field at the umpires and unruly fans ejected from the game. Nashville had loaded the bases with one out in the top of the seventh inning, only to have their man hit into a double play, causing mayhem in the Cakes' fans' seats.

Then in the bottom of the ninth, a double, a walk and a hit batter loaded the bases. Ten thousand fans were on their feet, standing in dead silence as the Cakes' cleanup hitter slowly strode to home plate, dramatically using his bat to knock the mud off his spikes. Two outs, two strikes and two balls, and the pitcher threw one high and inside, the wind from the pitch blowing the batter's helmet to the ground. The fans thought he'd been hit, which would have walked in the tying run, but the ump thought differently, causing loud cursing from the home team crowd.

"Boo! Boo! Kill the umpire," cried the New Orleans fans. The next pitch was another one inside, but the batter, who was now good and pissed, decided to step back and swing, knocking it over 400 feet into the center field bleachers, a grand slam out of the park that was infamous for allowing the fewest home runs in the league. All hell broke loose, even in the suite where all cheered a team that neither Jacques nor Paulette had ever heard of before that day.

CHAPTER 26

BACK AT THE COMPOUND THAT EVENING, WHILE
Nicky and Jacques discussed their plans for the future of the United States
of America, Johnny and Paulette went for a moonlight ride, one of the
boss's men following far enough behind so as to be unobtrusive and give
the couple space to be alone.

As a horseman, Johnny was not in her league, but he held his own.
The excitement of the ball game and the huge full moon over Lake
Pontchartrain made her romantic and, at one point, she stopped and
climbed over from her horse onto his, facing him in the big Western saddle
he'd chosen, her legs wrapped around his. She pressed her body to him
and kissed him deeply, making them both wish the guard wasn't around.

"I wish we could make love right here, baby," she whispered, "I want
to do it with you right on the ground, so I can smell the magnolias while
we fuck."

She plucked the state flower from a nearby tree and put it in her hair
and kissed him again. "God, I fucking love you, Johnny Santoro."

They turned their mount around and slowly walked him back to the
stable, the saddleless Palomino trailing behind. Antoine put the horses
up while they slipped into the house and past the room where her father
and his uncle talked business, and then to their room to make sweet love.

Dawn came hours later, and she wanted him again and the sight of her naked beauty as she lifted the sheet over them like a tent was almost more than his heart could bear. Benny Spellman's "Lipstick Traces" could be heard from a radio somewhere in the house as they made love with the early morning sunlight flooding the room and warming their bodies.

"Everybody up, it's already six o'clock," cried Nicky, "We gonna have some fun today!"

The man knew how to entertain, no doubt about it.

"We gonna meet up with ol' Landry over in Rayne. You all ever been to a Cajun festival?"

Jacques wiped the sleep from his eyes. He had as much stamina as most other men in their mid-40s, but he was finding it difficult to keep up with this 98-year old demon.

"Where's Rayne, Nicky?" he asked, still rubbing his eyes.

"Just a little over two hours' drive from here, so get your asses outta bed. Shower and shit and wear your sloppy clothes. Carmine's makin' us a little something for the ride, so we can have a bite in the car. This gonna be the most fun you ever had in your life!"

Fifteen minutes later, they were piled into the Escalade, followed by a second one carrying two of Nicky's men in case protection might be needed, and off to George Landry's house on the bayou in Rayne, "The Frog Capitol of the World," a town of roughly 8000 mostly Cajun people, due west of Metairie via Interstate 10. It was home to such local Cajun musicians as the late and legendary Harry Choates, Jo-El Sonnier, Johnnie Allan and Tony Thibodeaux, some of whom were scheduled to be on hand today to perform at the annual Frog Festival, attracting thousands of visitors, more than doubling the population of the small town.

Nicky always got the biggest kick out of Coon-asses, the name Cajuns had given themselves to distinguish their breed from descendants of the original French colonists who came to colonize Louisiana in the 17th century. The Cajuns, on the other hand, had come down from Acadia, or

French Canada, when the British conquered it and granted them the right to leave. They wound up in the Southwestern part of the state, where, to this day, they retain their quirky version of the French language in a dialect that has remained virtually unchanged for over 200 years. Nicky's own thick accent was that of his city of birth, a combination of gutter Sicilian and Southern black dialect, that less sophisticated ears sometimes confuse with Brooklynese. Unable to hear the humor in his own dialect, he found the accent of Landry's Cajun English to be hilarious, and he could hardly keep from laughing anytime he heard it spoken, no matter what foul mood he happened to be in.

He liked these people, although he recognized they were not at all the rubes or hicks many outsiders foolishly took them for at their own risk. He always said, "When I'm in them bayous, baby, I always keep one hand on my wallet."

They pulled into Landry's driveway a little before 9 am. Born into a family of church going alligator hunters, George had long ago crossed over to the dark side, hooking up with Nicky during the years when Carlos Marcello was away in prison. He worked his way up in the organization until he was now in charge of all mob activities, north, up to Baton Rouge, Monroe and Alexandria, and west into East Texas, in addition to traditional Cajun country, reporting—and paying tribute—to Nicky Santoro.

Landry showed them the huge head of the largest alligator ever caught in *Bayou Queue de Tortue*, a sixteen-foot monster that had outrun and outfoxed the Landry clan for two generations until George's father and uncle Troy had finally triple-hooked and put a bullet between the monster's eyes that day. It hung on the wall of his man cave, as his wife, Rose, refused to allow it in any other room of the house.

They caravanned to the fairgrounds, where the sounds of C.J. Chenier and his Red Hot Louisiana Band could be heard from one of the stages. C.J. was the son of the late, great Clifton Chenier, the King of Zydeco. The Creole musician was playing his accordion and singing his father's "Ay-Tete

Fee," a misspelling and mispronunciation of the bastardized French "*Ay Petite Fille*," or "Hey Little Girl." Clifton's biggest "hit," it had the crowd already jumping this early in the morning.

The blended aroma of Cajun and Creole cooking permeated the air. Nicky told George, "Take me to ol' Lee Mayeux, Landry. I need me some of that alligator sausage he makes."

Mayeux was also known throughout the bayous for his alligator gumbo. Landry had a standing order to bring some of either one to the old man once a week, "Because the protein makes my dick hard," he claimed. Although the harvesting of alligator eggs was illegal, or perhaps because it was, Nicky liked Landry to bring a few of those as well. He purchased one of Mrs. Mayeux's handmade alligator skin handbags for Paulette. Her husband tried to refuse payment, but Nicky slipped a one hundred dollar bill into the pocket of his wife's apron anyway.

Louisiana women tend to be good looking and the women at the fair grounds that day were no exception, "especially the big-leg fat ones," Landry bragged. His wife Rose weighed over 200 pounds. Even among these pretty women, Paulette stood out in her white angel blouse and torn blue jeans. Local hero, Jo-El Sonnier was now onstage and, after one look at her, he began to sing the old Harry Choates anthem, "*Jole Blon*," and had the entire crowd singing the girl's praises in Cajun French. Two large men lifted her up to the stage, where she stood next to the singer, embarrassed, but smiling as her father and Johnny proudly watched. Nicky too, felt a measure of pride, as he'd developed a fatherly affection for the soft-hearted girl.

Sonnier finished the song and said over the mic that he didn't recognize her and asked where she was from. "Old Greenwich, Connecticut," she confessed.

"Connecticut? You mean they got Yankee gals as pretty as you up north, *cher*?"

She blushed and answered, diplomatically, "Not as pretty as those I've seen in Louisiana," eliciting a huge cheer from the audience.

"Well, young lady, I'm going to name you an honorary Coon-ass," to the approving roar of the crowd. "You a for sure genuine star, darlin'," and men shoved each other aside for the privilege of helping her down from the platform. Then, recognizing Johnny, Jo-El said, "Well, hot damn! I shoulda known. Only the great Johnny Santoro could've brought him a *petite fille* like this one. You wanna play some, boy?"

Knowing that to decline would have been the height of rudeness, he hopped up onstage and took the guitar offered to him and kicked off the old Doug Kershaw song, "Louisiana Man," and the crowd went berserk, dancing and singing along.

The music, dancing, drinking and eating went on until late in the night. At the end, a sweet-voiced singer in an unnamed band sang that greatest of all Louisiana slow dance tunes, Art Neville's "All These Things," as Paulette and Johnny swayed slowly to the beat, clinging to each other for dear life.

Everyone slept on the ride back to Metairie. Everyone except Nicky, whose active mind never seemed to quit. He'd met his goal for the weekend, which was to insure that Jacques de Saint Marie was now blended into the Family. It was a goal he was certain he had achieved.

CHAPTER 27

A MONTH LATER, AROUND THE MIDDLE OF October, with only three weeks to go until the special election, it felt just like you'd want Indian Summer to feel in Connecticut. Temperatures in the northeast were in the high 70s and the Democrats were using it to hype global warming as a reason to vote for their candidate, assuming they could ever settle on one.

Both parties had mediocre line-ups to choose from. The Dems were again squabbling over whether to pick one of the old standbys, like Sanders, Hillary, Warren or even Biden. But even the most partisan voters ho-hummed, viewing them as a bunch of irrelevant old has-beens. Michael Moore tossed his dirty baseball cap into the ring, but the wiser Party elders blew him off, remembering how they'd blasted Trump for his weight and fearing they might look like hypocrites if they ran their fat guy, even allowing for the public's notoriously short memory.

They considered running another Hollywood celebrity, but had trouble coming up with a viable one, as most of the biggest names had died in the nuclear blast that destroyed the movie star capitol. And the smarter party consultants remembered how foolish they looked after nominating Sarah Silverman, given how she turned out.

For their part, the Republicans' bench was just as pitifully light on star power. Rubio, Cruz and Jeb each placed a tentative toe into the water, but the public just wasn't biting. As for a celebrity candidate, they had no one willing to run above the level of a Kid Rock or a Gene Simmons of the old 1970s costume rock band Kiss. Kanye West was mentioned briefly, but the idea of a Kardashian in the White House brought back too many memories of Donald J. Trump.

In fact, this was the problem across the board. Between the gossip-mongering media, always looking for a scandal to generate clicks, and the opposing parties' ability to find trash on just about anybody, any worthwhile possibilities simply weren't interested in having their dirty laundry aired.

The best the Republicans could come up with was a little-known senator from a sparsely populated plains state. She was a decent, wholesome Midwestern sort who loved her husband and family. Her record in the Senate was impeccable. She was always open to bipartisan solutions to the issues put before her and willing to compromise, despite her strong personal beliefs. She was pro-life yet unwilling to support laws prohibiting abortion, which was practically the only issue the average mal-educated voter cared about, or even understood in the slightest. One of those emotional issues that no one seemed to be able to address with any sense of logic or cool-headedness.

One GOP big shot even had the bright idea to offer O.J. Simpson up for nomination. "Hell, why not? Nobody thought Trump could be elected. Have you seen the way people crowd around O.J. to take selfies with him? They love this guy." Fortunately, cooler heads prevailed before word of this stupid idea leaked out to the press.

Nicky had moved quickly in the intervening weeks, lining up The Rock's people and hiring the best publicists he could find who were not affiliated with either of the two main parties. He decided to eschew the better-known political consultants and take control of things himself. With his ear always to the ground, no one had a better sense of the pulse of the American public than he did.

And he saw things in his boy's favor. For one thing, this was not a year for the fringe nuts. Ratings for Fox, CNN and MSNBC were in the toilet. Nobody was listening to the predictable Rachel Maddow or Sean Hannity anymore. Snarkmeister Steven Colbert's numbers were worse even than reruns of *Friends* at 11:30 at night. Politics were beneath everyone's radar. When Jimmy Fallon went out on the street and asked people who they liked for president, the answers ran from "Who's running?" to "There's an election?" to "Who gives a shit?" The mood in the country was moderation. Tired of all the nasty bickering, those who still voted at all were looking for someone at or near the center, someone neither party was able to offer.

To Nicky's way of thinking, it was the perfect storm for his candidate. At least most people had heard of him. Plus, he was a good-looking son-of-a-bitch. Combined with Handsome Tony, it was the most telegenic pair of running mates in history. He knew the key to winning was to get as much television exposure as possible for these two handsome specimens. So, he ordered the publicists to book them on any show at any time of day or night.

The level of questioning ran from the predictably inane to the imbecilic, which was exactly what Nicky wanted. Cable TV hosts looking to increase ratings by encouraging controversy, soon found they were barking up the wrong tree. Days passed without one inquiry as to either of their policy positions on any issue. It was all about charisma, personality and looks, all of which both men had in spades.

Skootching with Vito in New York, he quipped, "We might not even have to pull the shit we did for Kennedy in 1960. That double-crossin' Irish fuck."

"Yeah," Vito replied, "Remember that shit? In Chicago, we had more dead people voting than live ones. Them was the days."

"My people on the street tell me there is less than zero voter interest in this election, which is good for our side. Most of the assholes vote by habit. They'd vote for parakeet if it was runnin' in their party. They all so fuckin' stupid."

"Same damn thing here," Vito agreed, "The guineas vote for the guinea, the micks vote for the mick, the kikes vote for the kike and *tizzones* vote for the *tizzone*. Every fuckin' time. It never fails."

"Right, and then they stand there, callin' each other racist. Good thing they so stupid," Nicky laughed, "That's why you and me is rich."

Over the past two decades or so, politics had gotten uglier than ever. The Internet allowed even the most ignorant Americans to post the most outrageous, hateful garbage, most of it untrue, on social media, Twitter, Facebook and the like, as if it had any merit whatsoever. A gullible public was open to believing only what they wanted to hear, the things they already believed and equally open to disbelieve that which they didn't wish to know. The result being, as Nicky was prone to say, "Ain't nobody knows nothing."

CHAPTER 28

AFTER A QUICK TRIP TO PARIS, WHERE JACQUES
had arranged discrete financing for the election campaign, arrangements
were made to surreptitiously transport the money to the United States. It
wasn't as if one could just Fed-Ex bundles of hundreds of millions of dollars
from France to America. The IRS was always on the lookout, especially
when the recipient had an Italian surname. Banque de Saint Marie could
not afford that kind of scrutiny.

The way it worked was, ten large Oshkosh wardrobe trunks containing the money were quietly placed aboard a company plane, which
was dispatched from Charles de Gaulle Airport in Paris to *Aeroport
International Jean-Lesage de Quebec* in French Canada. From there, they
were loaded onto a van and then smuggled by boat across the international
border on Lake Erie and dropped off at the island of Put-in-Bay. There,
they were hidden at a small hotel near Admiral Perry's Monument owned
by a Cleveland mob associate and held until another boat took them to the
mainland at Sandusky, Ohio in the dead of night. They were finally driven
the one thousand miles to New Orleans, where the money was to be used
to finance the campaign, under the auspices of Nicky Santoro.

In the old days, a good deal of that money, as much as one third,
would have been skimmed off the top and placed into several of the large
drawers built into the wall of Nicky's personal room that contained many

millions in ever-increasing cash. But now he had a higher purpose. He'd reached the stage of life where, seeing that the end was not that far off, he was honestly convinced the country had been far better off when he and his Mafia friends were in charge.

"Shit, we more honest than any of them god damn politicians. We at least do what we say we gonna do, and we steal a lot less too," he was fond of saying.

So, he put the money from Paris in a special place to keep it separate from his own ill-gotten gains, sort of a mob version of an escrow account. It was illegal for campaigns to be financed by money from foreign countries, even friendly ones like France, so care was taken to disguise its provenance, which was child's play for a man of Nicky's vast experience at fooling the IRS.

Jacques was no fool himself and was always careful of who he did business with, yet his every instinct told him this old hoodlum was on the level, at least in this case. And he wasn't wrong. With so much free publicity and airtime, the campaign was costing far less than had been anticipated. The Rock got cover stories in dopey magazines like *People* and could even be seen smiling from the covers of liberal magazines like *Vanity Fair*, beating out the Democrats' candidates. The polls were one-sided, ridiculously so. The Rock/Calabrese ticket was looking to be a shoo-in. So much so, that Las Vegas odds makers were predicting a landslide. Some bookies were at the point of refusing to take larger bets, and the election was still three weeks off.

When Jacques returned home to Old Greenwich, he and Nicky had a Skootch session. "I know it looks like we can't lose," said the old man, "but I've seen a winning horse, ahead by six lengths, take a fall and break his damn leg at the last turn. In this world, brother, anything can happen."

"Ordinarily, I'd agree with you, but the other two candidates combined are lower in the polls than our man, who is well over fifty-five percent. I'm not breaking out the Dom Perignon Charles & Diana 1961 just yet, but I am keeping a corkscrew nearby, my friend."

Nicky chuckled, but deep inside, he always expected, and prepared for, the worst. He hated being disappointed but had to admit to himself that this election sure looked to be in the bag. All the signs pointed to an easy victory.

They disconnected and Jacques decided to head over to the club for eighteen holes with a few friends, while Nicky checked with his people to see what the latest poll numbers were since he'd last called less than an hour earlier.

As he wasn't needed to act as Tony Calabrese's traveling companion, Johnny gave himself permission to head up to Connecticut to be with Paulette for some R and R. Although her parents made him feel welcome to stay at their home, he hated feeling like a freeloader, so he made arrangements to spend part of the time at the home of Pete and his mother.

His insurance settlement hadn't come through yet and he still had no place to call his own. He hadn't even made up his mind where he wanted to live. LA was obviously out. So much for California. Too many unhappy memories and, anyway, the only other place he liked there was San Diego or, excuse me, Puerto de La Raza. Nope, fuck California. His last employer, Bonnie Raitt, was still so devastated that her people were saying she might never want to work again, which may have been a wise decision, as the majority of her fan base was on the wrong side of the age requirement for Social Security and no longer went out as often as when they were young.

The weather was still unseasonably warm and Paulette wanted to go to the beach in Stamford. The shore there was rocky, but they found a sandy spot big enough to spread their blanket and lay out in the warm sun with a cooler full of drinks, fruit and sandwiches from a nearby deli. The morning mist had burned off and Long Island was just barely visible across the water in the distance.

Gifted with her mother's long legs, she looked sensational in her bright blue bathing suit. Her bikini bottom was cut as low in front as the law in that state would allow, low enough to reveal that she was a fan of the Brazilian wax method. She looked positively tantalizing.

Admiring her from off to the side as she stood there, looking out at the Sound with her feet in the water up to her ankles, he asked himself whether it was the cut of her bikini top or had her breasts always been this full. He also noticed her stomach protruding slightly and it reminded him of all that good Cajun food they'd eaten at the Frog Festival. He'd developed a slight paunch himself. She returned to the blanket and as they lay there, close together, he gently rubbed her belly, as one would a favorite puppy, and she responded by whispering, "I don't know what it is, but all I want to do lately is fuck the living shit out of you." She looked into his eyes like she meant every word. She took a towel and, laying it over his body, placed her hand on his crotch, giving it a good squeeze.

"Now how do you expect me to walk down to the water like this in front of all these people, huh?"

He lifted her hand and kissed it, as if she were the Queen of England and he her most loyal subject. Before long, he was able to stand up and head down to the cool salt water with her for a little dip.

CHAPTER 29

HALLOWEEN WAS IN THE AIR AND KIDDIES
everywhere were once again permitted to dress up as ghosts, witches or
goblins, now that there were no current political figures unpopular enough
for parents to express their loathing by forcing their children to mock in
costume the figures they hated. Thankfully, that trend had become *passe*.

The political climate could now be best described as benign indifference.

With only a week to go until the election, Dwayne Johnson's latest
action flick was doing well at the box office. His talk show appearances,
even on the news channels, consisted of inane chatter about the movie as
interviewers swooned over how the special effects department got those
"awesome" shots of him leaping from one snow-covered cliff to another,
while holding the heroine in one arm and his trusty AK-47 in the other,
all to the sound of vintage Wu-Tang Clan on the soundtrack. The attitude
was more like, "Oh, and he's running for president too."

Most people never stop to consider the simple, obvious fact that these
men—and women--who seek to hold the highest office in the land, all have
enormous egos. The audacity to believe one's self capable of possessing the
qualities necessary to become the leader of the free world, would require
a narcissistic personality disorder, beyond any concept of narcissism a
normal person could imagine.

While he had to have a fairly healthy ego to have survived and prospered in the fields of sports, wrestling and movie stardom, Johnson's was not outlandish when compared to the usual pack of presidential hopefuls. He was actually the perfect candidate for the times, in the sense that his life was without scandal. There was nothing in his past that could be used to defame him, which meant both parties' typical tactics of trashing opponents' morality or ethics were of no use against him. And since their candidates had nothing of substance to offer policy-wise, they were at their wits' end, trying to think of things to say, and in interviews, often came off as tongue-tied.

The interviews with Tony were mostly about how great his hair looked, now that he'd begun to let a little grey show or which toothpaste he used to make his teeth so white. He always managed to find a way to modestly include a few words about how he'd led the way to the capture and arrest of the infamous Grid Hacker, while making sure to credit "those brave souls in our nation's law enforcement whose tireless work keeps our citizens safe from harm."

He'd developed a slightly annoying habit of introducing a new favorite word on some days. Today's was *elucidate*. "I'd like to elucidate here, that all the real credit for the capture and arrest of the perpetrator should go, not to me, but to the fine work of the men and women of the Federal Bureau of Investigation." But, since most voters were semi-literate at best, the *faux pas* sailed right over their heads.

One had to admit, Handsome Tony Calabrese may have been a bullshit artist supreme, but he was a charming rascal who knew how to milk this thing for all it was worth.

To most people, Election Day basically meant a day off from work or school. After the novelty of voting for a popular comedian in the last election wore off and having nothing new or "cool" to protest, the teenagers the Democrats had hoped would become their new constituency mainly spent their day off at the movies or playing video games. Or getting high.

At the end of the credits in Dwayne Johnson's movie, audiences saw a video of LL Cool J rapping a line composed by Nicky himself,

Do not hate, do not mock, hey everybody, vote for the Rock.

Of those few sophomoric young people whose brain cells could hold a thought for more than twenty seconds, maybe 10% of them showed up at the polls and virtually all of those who did clicked for the popular film star.

With no melodrama and hysteria to attract viewers, CNN, Fox and MSNBC all had the lowest ratings in electoral history. Even Chris Matthews, fired from MSNBC and reduced to a cheesy podcast viewed by no one, had no tingle up his leg. The more cynical viewers with too much time on their hands found innovative ways to enjoy the non-spectacle, watching with friends over the phone and making fun of the futile attempts of talking heads searching in vain for something exciting, or at least halfway interesting, to fill the time between commercials for cheap cell phones, catheters and My Pillows.

"Quick, check out Anderson Cooper, trying to pretend it's still a big deal to elect a black president. That's so 2008. Get a clue, Dude, it's 2021!"

"Oh wait, that idiot Hannity's acting like that chick senator from Bumfuck, Kansas still has a chance to win. She's, like, 20 points behind even the Dem…and Geraldo's actually agreeing with him!"

"Eew! Maddow's having another meltdown! She's freaking out because she can't think of anything to snark about. Get a fucking grip, bitch!"

Three hours before the polls closed, both the Republican and the Democratic hopefuls had conceded victory to the new President-elect, Dwayne Douglas Johnson, and publicly offered their tepid congratulations. Unlike in recent elections, the losers showed a modicum of class and nary a hint of the bitterness and resentment the public had become accustomed to. After all, they'd had plenty of time to get used to the likelihood of defeat.

Nicky, for reasons given earlier, had wanted the first post-election interview to go to Dana Perino, but clearer minds prevailed and Fox's Chris

Wallace was chosen instead. Arguably the best interviewer on television, Wallace had his hands full, asking the Rock, "How does it feel to be the first third-party president since Teddy Roosevelt?"

"It was real sad, what happened in Chappaquiddick."

"Uh, that was Teddy Kennedy, sir."

"Oh, yeah, right. You know, my movie, *Rampage 3*, jumped to number one at the box office this morning."

"Well, congratulations, Mr. President-elect, and we wish you and Mrs. Rock all the very best. Please come back and see us real soon."

Cut to commercial.

Tony had the hots for Megyn Kelly, and so she got him as a consolation prize, which was still a big "Fuck You" to her green-eyed colleagues at NBC's *Today* show whose envy over the increase of her already enormous salary caused them to loathe her beyond all loathing.

Both interviews came off as well as might be expected, each man glowing with positivity and showing unbridled optimism for the nation's future, all without saying much of any substance.

Mere victory was not enough for a man like Nicky Santoro, though. He rightly sensed that, for his team to have the kind of lasting impact he desired, they needed a signature issue, preferably one that would make one side happy without incurring the ire of the other. He needed something everyone could get behind.

He'd been working on something all along or, rather, had his nerd kids working on it. So far, they hadn't come up with an answer to the question that was on the minds of anyone who hadn't blocked it in order to remain sane. Neither his nerds nor the government's top investigators had been able to uncover which entity was behind the bomb that had destroyed the former city of Los Angeles and everyone in it.

Russia, Iran, North Korea, China, even Cuba had all been eliminated from suspicion. The Obama administration had posed no serious threat to any of these, but the unpredictable and volatile Trump had them fearing reprisal and instant destruction, had they dared to use even a small dirty bomb on an American city. The usual raft of terrorist groups would have been quick to take credit had any of them done the deed, so check them off. The Mexican drug cartels were also excluded from the list of bad actors; it simply wasn't their style.

Nicky told the kids to keep digging and meanwhile, had Tony order the speechwriters to come up with something on the subject.

CHAPTER 30

SINCE THERE WAS NO OUTGOING ADMINISTRATION, it was deemed advisable to hold the Inauguration as soon as possible, rather than wait for the traditional January date. Two weeks was rushing things, but it was felt they could put it together in that amount of time, with the help of the city's top professional party planners.

In the interim, the Rock flew to New Orleans to meet with his new vice president at the latter's home in the city's Lakeshore district. The route through the neighborhood took him past dozens of Mediterranean-styled palaces, each seemingly in competition for the prize for the gaudiest display of flashing Christmas lights that were traditionally lit up the day after Halloween each year. These, and the larger-than-life mangers, complete with life-like statuary of Mary and Joseph, along with the three Magi, all gazing down at the baby Jesus himself, little ducks, geese, lambs and goats looking on in wonder at the tiny Son of God. The best seller in local shops this year seemed to be a motorized infant whose little arms and legs wiggled about in the straw. Christmas songs, ranging from "Silent Night" to Nat "King" Cole's "The Christmas Song" to Charles Brown's "Merry Christmas Baby" and "White Christmas" by the Drifters rang out through the area.

Once behind the six-foot wall, he was immediately struck by the sight of the life-size, colorfully painted statue of the Blessed Virgin, amidst a garden of flowers in the front yard, her hands folded in prayer as a fountain sprouted gallons of water at her bare feet. Off to the left side of the walkway, was another statue, this one of Saint Agetha, the patron saint of Sicily and a particular favorite of Tony's wife, Arlene, who'd admired and prayed to the martyred virgin since childhood. Like the sainted Agetha, Arlene, too, had been untouched by man when she married her husband and was proud of the fact that no other man had ever had her "in that way" during the many years of their long and happy marriage.

Entering the ostentatious home, the president-elect noted the porcelain holy water font in the vestibule and, passing an image of St. Anthony, his curiosity was further aroused by the various religious artifacts within his purview, a large, wooden crucifix on the left wall in the dining room and, opposite, a painting of Our Lord, His eyes watching over the guests who came to dine. At a place of prominence in the living room was a large, engraved plaque, commemorating the Calabrese's audience with Pope Francis himself in 2016.

Transparent plastic runners marked the path on his tour from one room to the next until, finally, he was invited to have a seat on the plastic-covered Louis XVI chair of honor in the living room, next to a two foot-high, golden crucifix on an end table. Dressed for the occasion in Christmas-y red and green, Arlene Calabrese was quick to inform the president that the cross had come to her, at no small price, from an old church in Boston that had been desanctified and torn down in the wake of pedophilia charges aimed at the church's pastor. On another end table at the opposite end of the couch, was a crystal box containing what purported to be a portion of the True Cross, according to the engraving on the brass plaque at its base.

Arlene, excited over having the new President-elect of the United States of America in her home, was practically beside herself, and trying hard not to engage in the sin of pride. She handed him a plastic jar containing holy water from Our Lady of Lourdes that she'd had shipped for the occasion of his visit, "all the way from France, Mr. President, special for you to keep there in the Oval Office. It'll protect you from them slimy politicians you gonna have to deal with on a day-to-day basis." As she scurried off to attend to the running of her household, plans were made by the two men to visit Nicky Santoro that night. This would require a strategy worthy of the Normandy invasion.

Nicky's men, plus a large contingent of the city's finest, would block off side streets along the route to the compound to insure they wouldn't be spotted, not that paparazzi would be much of a factor in New Orleans. Once there, they were led to the lead-lined room built for secret meetings of this sort. After introductions and small talk, they got down to business. The President-elect spoke first.

"I have to confess, fellas, I never expected to win this thing. I'm scared to death; I don't know the first thing about this job. I'm used to being given a script to read to make it look like I know what I'm doing."

"And that's exactly what you'll be doin' now. We'll give you the words, and you'll say 'em. Tony here knows everything there is to know about this job. He'll put together your cabinet and guide you through every decision you'll be making. All you gotta do is smile pretty and say as little as possible."

"No disrespect, but this isn't the first time in our history the president has been essentially a figurehead," said Tony. "And it ain't the first time a vice president called the shots. So don't worry, I got your back. You're gonna do just fine. The people love you and they'll be very forgiving."

Nicky added, "Your speeches will be written. Just read off the teleprompter and there'll be no Q&A. Leave the questions to your press secretary. I been doing this a long time and I know what makes people tick. You're just what they need right now to pull this country together. All you have to do is do what you told and you'll make a great president. Trust me."

A few days later, on the Capitol steps, Dwayne Douglas Johnson was sworn in as the 47th president of the United States. He kissed his wife for the cameras and gave a short, stirring speech of hope for the future written by Peggy Noonan, one of the all-time best presidential speechwriters who'd written thousands of inspiring words for Ronald Reagan.

That night, Jacques and Patricia handed their invitation to the Inaugural Ball to one of the men at the door of the Washington Convention Center. They were seated at the new vice president's table and introduced to President Johnson as his largest donor, eliciting the Rock's brightest smile of the evening. As a tribute to Tony, the alternating band was one from his hometown that played traditional New Orleans jazz classics associated with the likes of Jelly Roll Morton and Louis Armstrong, "King Porter Stomp" and "West End Blues," among them, closing out the evening with Satchmo's "What A Wonderful World."

The morning after the ball, the couple took off for a much-needed vacation on the island of St. Croix in the U.S. Virgin Islands, where they spent the next two weeks at a tiny, six-room hotel called the Strand, on the leeward side of the island in a village called Frederiksted. Jacques preferred it to St. Thomas and even Christiansted, St. Croix's main town, for its privacy and lack of noisy, sunburned tourists. When the children were young, they had gone there as a family and had fond memories of the warm, crystal clear waters where Jacques and Pierre spent their days scuba diving. By the time they left, they were thinking of purchasing a winter home in the quaint, unpretentious little town.

With her parents away for Thanksgiving, Paulette was at loose ends and Pete invited Johnny and her to have dinner at his mom's house. Carole had called Johnny the day before to say her boss, Mr. Griffin, had some news about his insurance claim and could he stop by the office when he had a chance.

Griffin welcomed him with a smile and a friendly arm draped over his shoulder. "I have something for you I think you're going to like, Johnny," and handed him an envelope containing a company check for two and a half million dollars. His house, for which he'd paid less than four hundred thousand some twenty years before, turned out to have been worth one point nine at the time of the blast. The remainder was for his vinyl and instrument collections, his vintage 1959 Cadillac Eldorado plus an old life insurance policy he'd forgotten he'd kept up on his ex-wife and children.

"Of course, some of this will go toward paying off your mortgage."

"I don't have a mortgage, Mr. Griffin. I'm Italian; we don't buy anything on time."

"Then enjoy your money, my friend. I know it'll never take the place of your emotional losses, but it will help you make a new start. And please give my best to Jacques."

They shook hands and Carole walked him out to the elevator.

"See you and Paulette on Thursday, Johnny. Don't bring any food; Mom likes to do all the cooking."

"Okay, see you there, Carole, and thanks for everything."

They hugged and the door closed.

On the drive to Paulette's, he pondered what to do with his windfall. His needs weren't great, as he'd never been one to throw money around indiscriminately.

"At your age, you should only make conservative investments," she said when they talked later, "so your money will grow, slowly but with minimal risk, then maybe buy yourself a house. Renting is just throwing money away."

"You sure know your way around a dollar, don't you, baby?"

"Duh, you forget whose daughter I am? Listen to me and I'll have you set for life."

That was the most adorable thing any woman ever had said to him, he thought a few minutes later, as he stood in the bathroom, emptying his bladder. "It feels so good to know somebody gives a damn," he caught himself saying out loud.

While Jacques and Patricia were enjoying a Caribbean Thanksgiving dinner of Pavochon turkey, sweet yams, corn pie and pumpkin rice, dinner for their daughter was more traditional fare: roasted turkey, Honey Baked ham, mashed potatoes and gravy, sweet potatoes, green beans, cranberry sauce and lots of Betty's secret recipe corn bread stuffing. A veritable carnival of carbs. Dessert was pumpkin pie and ice cream and, of course, Betty's famous apple pie. As they did every year, Betty and Carole had spent the morning feeding the poor and homeless down at the church, something Paulette vowed to herself would become her habit in the future.

After dinner, while Johnny and Pete went outside to walk off some of what they'd eaten, Betty took Paulette in her room for a little girl talk.

"So, baby, how far gone are you?"

"What? Who? Me?"

"I'm a mother, sweetie. Been one a long time. You can't fool me. Does your man know?"

"God, no! I wouldn't know how to tell him."

"And your mama?"

"Oh man, she'd freak!"

"Well you need to tell him. That's his baby too. When are you due?"

"I don't know. I haven't seen a doctor yet. I just missed my second period."

"Hmm, judging from the size of those titties, I'd say two, two and a half months is about right. Now you get you to a doctor, and quick. And you tell Johnny too. If you need anything at all, I'm here for you, okay?"

"Thank you, Betty, I guess I've just been in denial."

"Honey, De Nile is nothing but a river in Egypt. You do what I tell you. Everything's going to be all right. That man loves you, whether he knows it or not. And I know you love him."

Paulette started to cry. "I don't know what's gotten into me lately. I cry at the least little thing."

"That's your hormones. Just wait another month or two. They're going to make you half crazy, and not very easy to be around."

"I'm going to have this baby, Betty. But what if he doesn't want it? What if he says he's too old to be a good father?"

"Of course you're gonna have it. That baby was made from love. It's God's gift to you both. He might hesitate for a hot minute, but don't you let that bother you. He'll come around. I know him a long time and that's a good man."

When the guys came back from their walk, Betty and Paulette were at the sink, helping Carole with the dishes. Betty turned to Johnny and said, "Your girl's got something to tell you, so why don't the two of you go into my room and have yourselves a little chit chat?"

CHAPTER 31

ONE OF NICKY'S COMPUTER NERDS SENT A message that he had something "insanely important" to tell and needed to see him immediately. Twenty minutes later, they were sitting in the private room.

The kid, one of Nicky's sharpest, said he'd been watching a show on the History Channel that posited the theory that Adolph Hitler had not committed suicide in that Berlin bunker in April, 1945 but in reality had escaped Germany at the end of World War II, along with thousands of Nazis, and wound up with new identities in Argentina and other South American dictatorships. Knowing the war was all but lost, plans had been made throughout the previous year to shift operations across the Atlantic and to the south, with the intention of setting up a Fourth Reich. None of this was news to Nicky and he just shrugged his shoulders.

The kid had done more digging and managed to uncover information that revealed that in a factory in Norway, the Germans had been making "heavy water," or deuterium oxide, a main component in the making of a nuclear bomb.

Apparently, the port of Narvik in the north of the country was one of the places from which the Nazis launched their U-boats, the plan being to use these to ship large quantities of this heavy water to South America, with the intention of building a bomb that could annihilate the city of New York and conduct a future war against the United States on their own turf.

"So, Mr. Santoro, I was thinking, What if..."

"Yeah, yeah, I get it," he interrupted impatiently.

Nicky's razor-sharp mind was now working a mile a minute. Yes indeedy, what if those same subs had also been used to transport high-level Nazis, perhaps even Hitler himself, to Argentina? He already knew about the notorious Ratlines, the escape routes, complete with smugglers, guides and safe houses, through Austria and Italy that, some said, with the help of certain priests and even the Vatican itself, helped thousands flee to fascist-friendly South American countries, like Argentina under the iron-fisted dictator Juan Peron. To these later groups, the antiquated concept of an ideological right or left meant nothing, as what they were after was raw power.

Additionally, Nicky had been aware for some years of a secret network called Odessa, an organization of former SS members, founded in 1946 with chapters in Brazil, Chile, Bolivia, Uruguay and Paraguay. He already knew about *Die Spinne*, yet another group that had helped thousands of Nazis, including Josef Mengele under the alias Helmut Gregor, to escape via Francisco Franco's Spain and the Canary Islands, into South America under new identities supposedly provided by the Red Cross. When Peron was deposed, Mengele made his way to Paraguay, whose own dictator was one Alfredo Stroessner, a Nazi sympathizer who allowed the erstwhile dictator to live out his days in comfort in the small town of Asuncion where there was a large German consulate.

During the war, German U-Boats were stationed in the mid-Atlantic as refueling stations for large seaplanes that carried top-level Nazis and large caches of gold bullion to Buenos Aires, and eventually to jungle hideouts such as Bariloche and Misiones in the north where it was easy to assimilate into already existing sizeable German communities. Other Argentine cities with large German populations included Cordoba, Entre Rios, La Pampa and of course, Buenos Aires.

He had every reason to believe there was the possibility, even a likelihood, that German descendants of these war criminals might still be active in the hopes of realizing the dream of a Fourth Reich in the Western Hemisphere.

Significantly, Argentina was now the world's main producer of heavy water, with a plant located at Arroyito. If these modern-day Nazis indeed had access to this heavy water, it also meant they had both the means and the motive to destroy the city of Los Angeles with an atomic bomb as a first strike in a war of belated revenge against America.

"You did real good, kid. Now keep this quiet for now, but you and your friends keep digging and let me know every little detail of what you uncover, no matter how small."

He felt that this could be that signature issue he'd been looking for. If they were able to, not only uncover a cadre of Nazis in South America, but take them out, both the Rock and Tony would be heroes, guaranteeing, not only eight, but even sixteen years of presidents under the control of this Mafia/Freemason combine he'd skillfully put together. He knew he was unlikely to live that long himself, but that wasn't the important thing. What was important was that the legacy of *La Cosa Nostra*, this thing of ours, should live on, in perpetuity.

Filled with excitement, he texted Tony, telling him to come over as soon as possible, so they could formulate a plan of action.

"If I was them German fucks, what would I do?" Nicky mused aloud once Tony had heard the entire hypothesis.

Tony agreed, "Well, remember in 1939, they signed a pact with the Soviet Union when the two of them invaded Poland together. The partnership only lasted two years, until Hitler fucked Stalin *nel culo*, up the ass."

"He was a real *strunz*, that one, but it could've been either one done the fucking. You can't trust neither of them fucks, even today. If we do something, what we need to watch out for is if the South American Nazis hook up with the Russians. And don't think that can't happen, my friend."

"I know; a fucking Russian'll fuck his own mother if he can."

"What we need to find out, on the QT, is if there's any connection between them bastards already. My chirren dug deep into Russia on the net and found nothing suspicious, so I think we're okay there, so far. But we got to be sure."

"So now what?"

"Let me find out more. If it's them for real that did the bomb, you'll give the info to your friends at CIA and let them make out like they found out on they own. Who cares, let them take the credit. Then we'll let the media have it, to rile up public support. The president will make a big speech on TV, so congress will have no choice but to declare war. We take 'em out, and you're the biggest hero there ever was. Next election cycle, the Rock says he's stepping down for health reasons and because you deserve the office and, Bam, we got our first guinea prez."

"It sounds almost too easy, Nicky. There's got to be a catch, no?"

"They always is. The trick is gonna be, we got to find all the spots where they living, and that could be anywhere south of the equator. I hear they got bunkers in the fucking jungle, even. And who knows if the CIA has German-speakin' guys who can infiltrate, or German-lookin' guys who speak good Spanish? Lotta problems here, you know what I'm sayin'? Them damn Nazis is like a *cimici*, the hardest thing in the world to get rid of. But if it is them, then we got our work cut out for us, brother."

CHAPTER 32

BY THE CHRISTMAS SEASON, THE COUNTRY WAS in a good mood. With a non-partisan, post-ideological president who had no set bigger agenda, only the fringe characters on either the right or left had any complaints. But no one paid much attention to them because a) complaining is their default setting anyway and b) the Rock's personality was so upbeat and contagious that anybody who opposed him would only look foolish. This was the first time in decades that the Republicans and Democrats weren't at each other's throats. There was simply nothing to be gained for either party by being nasty.

It was left to Vice President Calabrese to speak to the public on anything of importance or that required improvisation. The president's role was limited to reading happy talk off teleprompters and smiling a lot. He was so popular that the press and the media didn't dare go after him as they had the last three full term commanders-in-chief.

In his speeches, Tony Calabrese took to inserting the occasional subtle hint about the progress being made in uncovering those who perpetrated the "LA tragedy," as it was now being called. Most people had begun to call cities like Los Angeles, San Diego and the others by their original names again, and even those curmudgeons who'd campaigned in favor of changing all names that could be taken as religious kept their objections to themselves. It was a time of contentment and optimism for all.

Behind the scenes, Nicky's internet nerds, along with investigators from CIA and the FBI were, separately and typically unknown to each other, working hard at tracking down Nazi connections in South America. This operation was delicate, because the continent was split into two opposing factions. In addition to the right-wing dictatorships, on the other side were the communist countries on the left like Venezuela, Cuba, Costa Rica, Nicaragua and others.

United States interests dictated that it was best to keep things in South America in balance. If one side were to become noticeably more powerful, war could erupt in the southern hemisphere and whichever one won would be disastrous for the U.S., because, despite American propaganda to the contrary, our nation did not have the military capability to conduct continent-wide operations. To defend against this kind of event, the CIA had for years put a lot of effort into surreptitiously manipulating and maintaining this delicate balance.

Now, they dispatched agents to countries with known Nazi sympathies to quietly sniff around. With money from Jacques' banking and Freemason connections, Nicky also sent some of his people, but, speaking no German and little Spanish, their actions were limited in scope.

What did manage to emerge from these investigations was a sense that certain of these groups were not at all unhappy with the destruction of an American city and the damage such an act had done to the nation's morale and the level of fear it had raised among her citizens. But it was difficult to know who exactly it was that felt this way. Nor were any of the experts able to discern whether it could be the Nazis or communists, both of whom hated America equally, and who might have done the deed. So, at least for the time being, no action, or reaction, was forthcoming.

CHAPTER 33

UNLIKE LESS SOPHISTICATED TOWNS, LIT UP LIKE
Times Square for the holidays, Old Greenwich eschewed such gaucherie
as Christmas lights and statuary. No Santa, no reindeers and sleigh, no
mangers, no Magi, no Baby Jesus, not even one electric blue menorah in a
living room window for Hanukkah as far as the eye could see.

Paulette's birthday, Christmas Eve, was coming up and she was now
showing. She'd told her mother, who wasn't at all shy about expressing her
opinions, especially in the presence of her husband who, like most men,
was extremely awkward discussing such sensitive matters. His solution was
to keep any opinions to himself and allow the women to do all the talking
in an attempt to keep the peace.

"Johnny is a decent fellow, Paulette, and I understand you want a father
in the picture. You think you love him, but marriage? Really? The man is
old enough to be your grandfather, for God's sake! What is the likelihood
of his even living long enough to see the child graduate high school? Are
you sure you even want to have this baby?"

"Mother, I am not even going to discuss aborting my child, so that
conversation ends right here. And as for Johnny, I have never known a
man as good and kind as him, not even you, Daddy. I love him with all
my heart and I'll take as many years with him as I can get. I am going to
marry him, and that's final."

"Jacques, can't you say something? Please! This is madness!"

"Now calm down, dear."

"Calm down? Calm fucking down, for Christ's sake? How can you say that to me?" And with that, Patricia stomped out and stormed upstairs to her room, slamming the door.

"Daddy, you know better than to ever tell a woman to calm down. That little remark is going to cost you a pair of diamond earrings, at least."

He sighed and said, "Okay, Paulette, I get it. You love him. I obviously think the world of him too, for all he did for us and for you. I genuinely like the man. But, has he even proposed?"

"Daddy, please! Please don't try and talk me out of it. I want to marry him. I am going to marry him!" She took a breath and said, "And don't be so old fashioned. I am a modern woman. I proposed to him."

"Sweetheart, if that's truly what you want, I will give you my blessing. And your mother will eventually listen to reason. I promise I'll get her to cooperate. If this is what will make you truly happy, I'll see to it."

With that, he went to his daughter and held her in his arms, leaning over to kiss the hair on the top of her head. She put her arms around him and said, "I love you Daddy. Thank you for understanding."

After dinner, she drove over to Greenburgh to see the father of her baby, to give him the news and convey her father's blessing, diplomatically omitting the part about her mother's fit of disapproval.

Pete's family was happy to see her and the women rubbed her belly for good luck and, generally, made a fuss over the young mother-to-be.

"How would one of you like to be the godmother?"

"Well, at my age, I might not be the best choice. You need someone who'll be around long enough to help raise him or her if need be," was Betty's sage advice.

"Think I'm young enough honey?" asked Carole, who was still in her late 40s."

"You betcha, Carole. I pick you."

"I'm honored, and I'll babysit too, whenever you want."

"You can count me and Mom in for that duty too, baby girl," Pete piped up.

Johnny had been out at the local BMW dealership, picking up his new car, a midnight blue, four-door 500 series, and walked in at the tail end of this conversation. Paulette jumped up, excited to tell what her parents had said, or at least what her dad had said, and suddenly felt something strange down below. She rushed to the bathroom and, looking between her legs, saw blood in the toilet.

"No! No!"

Betty heard and rushed in. "What's the matter, baby?"

The others stood in the doorway.

"I'm bleeding. What do I do? What's happening to me? Is my baby going to die?"

"Now, be cool, baby," said Betty, taking charge. "It's called spotting. We're going to take you to the Emergency and the doctor will tell us what's going on. Don't worry, just stay calm, cool and collected. Everything's gonna be copacetic. Pete, we'll take your car; we're all going together, like family."

Pete went out and started up the Cherokee and everybody piled in, Johnny in front and Paulette between the women in back, with a towel between her legs. It hadn't rained or snowed, so they made good time.

A doctor who was a friend of Carole's spotted her in the lobby and snuck Paulette in front of the line. Johnny was a nervous wreck so Pete walked him outside to try and distract him, while Betty and Carole sat wordlessly in the waiting area.

A half hour later, they were allowed in to see the patient. The doctor said that all looked well, no signs of polyps or infection. She said that spotting, or light bleeding, occurs in approximately 20% of pregnant women during the first trimester. It can be caused by changes in the cervix, making it softer and more prone to bleeding. Sometimes this happens following intercourse or a pelvic examination.

She gave her a package of panty liners and pads to wear so she could keep track of the amount of blood. "If it continues to happen, make sure you see your gynecologist right away, okay? If by chance the bleeding gets heavier, go immediately, but I don't think you have anything to worry about. Get plenty of rest and no strenuous activity. Keep the sex gentle. You have loving family around you, and that's key."

They all thanked her profusely and went back home to Betty's. Paulette called her mother to tell her what had happened and that she felt it best she stay the night at Betty's and not drive home until morning.

When Patricia relayed the information to Jacques, he told her, "I don't want you to feel guilty or that you are at all to blame, darling, but we can see it is incumbent that we give her all the love and support we can. I believe Johnny will stick by her. He's proven his feelings for her and, for as long as he has on this earth, I'm sure they'll be happy together. Can I count on you, dear?"

"Yes, of course. I just flew off the handle at the shock of it all and I'll apologize as soon as she gets home. I guess the notion of becoming a grandmother at my tender age was a little too much for me. Just don't let the child call me Grandma, please?"

"And what a beautiful grandmother you're going to make." Jacques knew his wife, and her vanity. A little flattery never failed to settle her nerves.

CHAPTER 34

"DO YOU LIKE OLD FRENCH MOVIES?" PAULETTE asked Johnny the following afternoon back in Old Greenwich.

"I can't remember ever seeing one," he admitted. "The only French I know is a little Cajun. I can understand some of what they're saying, but can't really speak it."

"There's two with Catherine Deneuve, playing in Stamford tonight. Will you take me?"

"Sure, I'll try anything. I can read the subtitles."

"I love her, especially when she's with Gerard Depardieu. They're showing their most famous one, *The Last Metro*, and my fave, *Choice of Arms*. Yves Montand is in it too, playing her husband, a retired gangster who now breeds horses."

"I know how you love horses. Sounds like a double winner for you, Boo. Yeah, let's do it."

"We can have dinner at Le Fat Poodle, right here in town first. It's a really nice French restaurant. It'll put us in the mood. I'll make a rez for six o'clock, so we can make the movie in time. It's def not fast food."

She felt like getting dressed up while she could still fit into her nicer dresses, so they got ready, then headed out, past the Innis Arden Golf Club, and on to the brasserie on Arcadia Road. Once inside, she was warmly greeted by the owners and led to a good table, as befitting the daughter of

Jacques de Saint Marie. On the way, she stopped to say hello and introduce Johnny to some of her parents' country club friends.

In the background was *"Ne Me Quitte Pas,"* being sung by Barbra Streisand. "Should we leave?" asked Paulette, seeing Johnny cringe at the sound of her voice.

"No, it's okay," he laughed, "She's no Nina Simone, but at least she sings in tune."

They were barely seated when their waiter, Andre, came over and said, "So lovely to see you again, Miss Paulette. Would you care to see a wine list?"

Rather than reveal that she wasn't drinking, due to her condition, she said, "No thank you, Andre, we have to catch a movie at eight, so we'll need to get in and out fairly quickly. If you can give us a few moments, we'll be ready to order."

Neither of them was that hungry so they decided to split a few things from the appetizer menu. He chose the grilled oysters, and she wanted tuna *tartare* and to share a beet salad. Inspired by what they saw on the table next to theirs, they split an order of steak frites with bordelaise sauce and *pommes frites*. They skipped dessert, as they didn't want to be late, taking two *crème brulees* to go.

By the time they parked and arrived at the old Avon Theatre in Stamford, the previews were already on and they made their way to seats in the back row. She told him, "This used to be a single theater but they split it into two smaller ones. But I still love it anyway. It's the only place around to see foreign or indie films."

First up, was *Choice of Arms*, in which man and wife, Yves Montand and Catherine Deneuve, live on a large estate outside of Paris. His criminal past catches up with him in the form of an old mobster friend on the run who arrives with a psychotic partner, played by Gerard Depardieu. Detectives eventually show up and Deneuve is accidently killed in a crossfire before the film is half over. It's hardly your typical gangster movie plot.

While the credits rolled, they went to the lobby to stretch their legs. He was reminded of how, due to his ex-wife's profession, he was always forced to sit through the endless roll of names he didn't know, as was the custom in Hollywood, where everyone is in the business and searches the credits for friends and acquaintances who might help advance their careers.

"How'd you like it? Wait till you see the next one, *The Last Metro*. It's even better. It's a historical drama that takes place during the German occupation of Paris during World War II. She and her husband own a theater, but the husband is Jewish and so she hides him in the basement."

"So, Depardieu plays the husband?"

"No, you'll see. He's an actor who's hired for a role in the theater's new production.

"She sure is beautiful, isn't she?"

"They call her *le Visage de la France*, the Face of France. I've seen dozens of her films. I could watch her for hours. She's a very minimalist actress, sort of like Robert Mitchum. Her face reveals so much with so little movement."

He found her enthusiasm contagious.

"I noticed that about her too. Don't laugh, but she reminded me of Count Basie, the way he plays so few notes, a plink here and a plunk there, but every note is just the right one."

Paulette laughed, getting exactly what he meant. "I love how we are so in tune with each other, don't you, baby? We like all the same things." Back at their seats, she draped one leg over his and laid her head on his shoulder.

The movie came on and, seeing Deneuve's tightly wound French twist hair-do, Paulette whispered, "Think you'd like me with my hair like that?"

"I'd like you if you didn't have one hair on your head."

"Good answer!"

A woman with a pinched-up face, a few rows in front of them turned around and said, "Shhh," and they stopped talking, struggling to suppress a giggle.

Snowflakes were beginning to fall, reflecting white in the glow of the streetlamps, as they walked back to the car later. Paulette asked, "So? Are you a fan of French films now? Did I convert you?"

"I do believe you did. But just don't ask me to see any Kung Fu flicks, okay?"

"Deal. Ain't gonna happen, my love. *Ma cher*. My Boo," she answered, attempting to mimic his New Orleans manner of speech.

A thin layer of snow covered the streets by the time they were back at her house. She went to the bathroom to check her panty liners for any more spotting. Seeing none, she sighed in relief and then held her hair up from behind to see how she'd look in Deneuve's twist. *I think I'll do it like this for my wedding*, she thought to herself, pouting at the mirror like a model she'd seen in an Yves Saint Laurent advertisement in the fashion magazine *Vogue*.

She pressed her ear to her parents' door and, hearing nothing, assumed they were asleep. Returning to her room, she said to Johnny, "I'm pretty tired, baby. Can we go to sleep now?"

He nodded and they got undressed, and brushed their teeth standing together at the bathroom mirror, her left hand pressed against the bare skin of his lower back.

"Baby, I even love brushing my teeth with you. It makes me feel so close to you."

He smiled and dabbed her nose with a dollop of toothpaste.

CHAPTER 35

NICKY'S CHIRREN HAD UNCOVERED WHAT SEEMED
to be a neo-Nazi sub-group of some kind. With the aid of a German-
to-English translation program, they were able to decipher suspicious
messages between a group in Buenos Aires and others in the cities of
Itapua and Nueva Germania in Paraguay. It was a difficult task, as the
messages often contained sentences and phrases that were a mix of German
and Spanish. But with the help of one of the girls who was fluent in both
languages, they were able to make notes and pass them on to Nicky and
Tony, who, seeing this job was too big for Nicky and his crew alone, got
together with General Colleen McQuarter to formulate a plan of action.

It appeared that neither Adolph Hitler nor any World War II era Nazis
remained alive, as the process of cryonics had yet to be proven viable, but
there did seem to be a resurgence in the ideology among a subsequent
generation possibly descended from German escapees of that earlier time.
From intercepted emails, they could see one of the group's main figures
appeared to be a woman named Helga Goetsch who seemed to be giving
orders to subordinates. While they saw no sign of her taking credit, it
was clear that she knew, and was at the very least pleased, even thrilled,
about the bombing of Los Angeles, although they turned up no substantial evidence that she was directly involved. The most frequent name on
emails to and from her was that of a man named Friedrich Forster, who

was constantly on the move, communicating from various locations in Paraguay, Uruguay and Chile.

Clearly, these were people who hated America, judging from phrases like, "When the American weaklings and the Jews who own them are wiped from the face of the earth," or after an Iranian mullah had made anti-Semitic threats on a BBC interview, "*Der Iran hat die Idee. Tote alle schmutzigen Juden.*"

"Politically speaking, there's no way we can just go in there and bomb the shit out of them," Tony told General McQuarter, "Or can we?"

"No sir, definitely not," she answered, "But let me put together a tactical study group. Maybe we can come up with something like we did during the Sandinista era. Combining CIA assets with Special Forces, to infiltrate if possible or at least find out how much sympathy there is for this Fourth Reich, we may be able to uncover what we're up against. Then send in Special Forces or Navy Seals to take out the leaders, once we know who they are. Right now though, it looks like there's just too many, too spread out. I mean, we're talking about all over god damn South America."

"Yeah, who knows if we can even put together enough locals to help us do the job? Or do the locals support these bastards? They've been there for almost seventy-five years now. They're part of the scenery by this time, right?"

"For now," the general said, "Let's keep this under wraps. With all due respect, sir, we can't depend on congress or the senate to know what to do, much less agree among themselves to do anything helpful. So, any leaks in that direction will only hinder our efforts."

"You right, General. Excuse my language, but those assholes I'm stuck with in those senate committees couldn't agree on a decision if they life depended on it. They so worried about getting reelected it's like they frozen stiff."

After she left, he thought it wise to confer with Nicky and fill him in on the meeting. Maybe he'd have some thoughts on the matter.

At that very moment, Nicky was in discussion with a young man named Ned, one of his brightest Internet experts, in the windowless room. Ned had stumbled upon something that he felt his boss would find very interesting. Seeing his hesitation, Nicky coaxed him, "Kid, you know by now you can tell me anything. This world is so strange these days, you never know what might lead to something."

"Okay then, here goes. In my tracking of these people down there, I happened to notice that the places they were messaging from are all in a straight line on the map. Not only that, but some of them are so far out in the jungle, there's no electricity, so I asked myself, how can they charge their computers or phones? I heard one of them mention something about a factory nearby, too."

"Go on, I think I got an idea where you goin' with this."

Squirming in his seat, but feeling more confident to continue now, Ned went on.

"Well, are you familiar with the theory that there are locations on earth where magnetic energy is especially powerful?"

"Yeah, I know all about that shit. A lot of them spots got temples or pyramids built on 'em, some more than ten thousand years ago."

"Right, and here's the thing. They're all situated along straight lines that go around the world, from one to the next."

"I know, I know, like a grid, right? I heard about that."

Despite the fact that he'd spent so much time in Nicky's company, Ned never failed to be impressed and even surprised at his boss's vast knowledge of esoteric information.

"Some people believe these grids were mapped out by, don't laugh, extraterrestrials as a way of transmitting energy."

"You see me laughin' kid? I know where you goin' with this. There was this German scientist, Wernher von Brown…"

"Braun."

"Whatever the fuck. He was way ahead of his time with rockets and all that stuff. After the war, I remember he was captured and our government made him work for us, and he came up with all kinds of space travel shit, right?"

"Yes, and his discoveries were so advanced, some believe he could only have gotten them from communicating with beings from another, advanced civilization. But the thing that struck me was this straight line, this grid, so I charted it on a map, north and south, and it runs up through Mexico, Yucatan and these ancient Mayan temples and on up into Arizona and places where the Zuni and Hopi tribes claim to have been visited by flying ships and what they call Star People thousands of years ago."

"Slow down, boy. So, you sayin' it's like a power grid and they don't need no wires for electricity? Wait a minute. How do they get Internet service in them far out areas?"

"With the advent of satellite Internet service, you can send and receive email anywhere on earth now."

"Well, ain't that some shit? And a factory, you say? In the jungle? That could be where they made an atomic bomb without being noticed."

"Yes sir, call me crazy, but I really think it's all plausible."

"You done good, son. An' you ain't crazy at all. Now keep lookin', and bring me everything you find, no matter how weird it sounds. We gettin' someplace now."

CHAPTER 36

AS SOON AS NED LEFT, NICKY TEXTED TONY THAT
he needed to see him in person ASAP. Tony knew, vice-president or not,
this was no request or mere suggestion. More than even before, he was
bound to his master, as long as the two of them remained breathing.

The hard part would be eluding the two gentlemen from the Secret
Service who dogged his every move. He knew they were there for his safety
but, in truth, he felt safer with the men provided by Nicky. Their loyalty
was undeniable. In Santoro world, disloyalty was a death sentence. Nicky's
solution was one he was fond of stating: "Everybody has they price." So, he
made sure Tony's Secret Service contingent was well compensated to stay
out of the way whenever he required privacy. Having served other politicians before him, they simply assumed he was off for a little romantic
rendezvous. Nicky's men and his connections at the New Orleans Police
Department took over from there.

So, Air Force Two was gassed up and headed for Louis Armstrong New
Orleans International Airport, where Vice-President Calabrese's Secret
Service security team handed him off to his friends on the NOPD, who
drove him in a pair of SUVs to the compound of Nicky Santoro.

Once in the private room, Tony said, "I hope this is important. With
these Secret Service guys always around, people gonna get suspicious if
you and me get together too often."

"I wouldn't of called you down here if it wasn't." He got right into it. "You get them, whachoo call 'em, briefings every morning, just like the prez, yeah? The top-secret shit?"

"Right, I know everything he knows. That's the deal."

"Okay, I been told for years that every president from at least Eisenhower on knows there's aliens and has been in contact. They told you about all that yet?"

"Yeah, I heard something 'bout that just the other day. Apparently, the contact ain't been all that often. Might not have been none since old Clinton."

"Kinda makes you wonder, why not the later ones? What if they seen how fucked up the country is and decided to switch sides? Don't that bother you, man?"

They regarded each other and Nicky then told him everything that Ned had deduced.

"What if," he continued, "them aliens figured the Nazis was a better bet to fit their plans, whatever they might be? You wasn't born yet, but in World War II, odd things kept going our way, like we got the atom bomb first, for example. Why? By the time of Viet Nam, we was fucking up bad and things been going downhill ever since. What if the aliens figured we was a lost cause and went over to one of the other sides?"

"Like the Nazis you mean?"

"That's what I'm talkin' about, brother. Them or the fuckin' communists. What the hell's the god damn difference?"

"Thing is, me and the Rock was told this is something we can never say to nobody, 'cause it could make people panic. They doing a slow reveal, with books and movies and TV shows that hint at it, to prepare the public for the possibility. They'll probably come clean in the next five years or so."

"Well, they might not have no choice if this Nazi thing down there in Argentina got any legs to it."

"You wanna hear something funny? Fucking Clinton, between that young pussy and his bull dyke wife always bustin' his balls to be his 'co-president,' had his mind so messed up he came this close to spilling the beans when he was in the White House."

They laughed, and Nicky said, "You think that's funny? Can you imagine if the two who came after him had contact with aliens? That pussy Obama would've handed over the country to 'em on a silver platter and that dumb ass Trump might've done something even worse, like try to fight 'em. Well, now it's up to us. You and me stay in contact every day, on the Skootch or the video games. They encrypted, so we can talk without nobody listening in."

"Meanwhile," Tony said, "on my end, I'll ask around and see if there's a way to make contact and let them know we don't want no problem with them. Or do you think they already know what we thinking, like through telepathy or something?"

"Ain't no way of knowing, son. Just keep your thoughts pure," he smiled.

They shook hands and Tony was out the door, and on his way back to the airport. At one point during his flight back, he woke up from a nap and thought he saw a flying object off the starboard side of the plane. It seemed to hover, very close to the tip of the wing, almost touching, then took off at an astonishing speed. He wondered if it had been a dream and considered asking the pilot if he'd seen anything strange, but then thought better of it and kept his thoughts to himself, thinking, *I'll bring it up at the next meeting with those NASA cats.*

CHAPTER 37

THE TWO FRIENDS ENTERED LA MANDA'S, AN OLD
school Italian restaurant on Tarrytown Road that had been there since
1947. The walls were made of the knotty pine that had been popular that
year. They were badly discolored, harkening back to a time when smoking
was allowed in restaurants. There was still a large, yellowing black and
white photograph of Babe Ruth and Lou Gehrig on the wall behind the bar
that Pete remembered from his youth and always made him feel nostalgic.
Several of the men at the small bar looked as though they'd been sitting
there on the same six stools since the place opened, gnarled, grizzled old
working men whose lineage from the tiny, mountain towns of Calabria
or Abruzzo was etched upon their craggy faces. Men who worked with
their hands, whose aching backs and knees told of many long hours laying
brick or fitting stone or repairing and replacing railroad ties in the cold of
winters or the stifling heat of too many summers.

One of those faces was that of old Nino Petrucci, who Pete recalled as
the groundskeeper at Metropolis, up Dobbs Ferry road. He remembered
Petrucci, who had seemed old even then, when Pete was a teenager carrying two bags of golf clubs, one slung over each shoulder. Nino drove around
the golf course on his lawn mower, the hot sun baking the olive skin on his
arms and face to a reddish brown, under the wide-brimmed straw hat he
always wore on his head. The whole of his life consisted of the club from

dawn till dusk, returning to his wife and five children each evening, after stopping off at La Manda's for a single cold glass of beer after work. Home, family and hard, outdoor work were his entire world, except for Sundays, when his wife prayed for his soul at the church of Our Lady of Mt. Carmel, while he played *bocce* ball with other men like himself. Even after decades as an American citizen, his English was still rudimentary at best, barely enough to convey his comprehension of what his employers expected of him, and little more. At home, he spoke in the dialect of the *Abruzzese*, as had generations of his ancestors in the mountainous western part of that province, known as *L'Aquila*.

Many American celebrities could trace their ancestry to Abruzzo, including the musicians Dean Martin, Perry Como, Henry Mancini, Michael Buble, boxer Rocky Marciano and even the entertainer Madonna, but these were names unknown to Petrucci. Popular culture held no meaning for men like him. What mattered was the growing cycles, how much to trim the grass on the greens, when and how much or how little to irrigate, in order to maintain a firm surface and to promote deep rooting. The right time of year to replace the metal cups in the holes which caught the little white dimpled balls of liquid, covered with urethane. Of these things, Nino Petrucci was a master, a savant, despite the fact that he was unable to read or write a word of either English or his native tongue. He nodded, unsmiling, to Pete as he and Johnny passed by on their way to a wooden booth by the long window, beneath the sign that read "Pizzaria, Lounge, La Manda's Restaurant, Bar" in blue and red neon.

One half hour later, Johnny was finishing his order of *scarparo*, chicken in a sauce of garlic, white wine, butter and vinegar, and Pete was enjoying the last traces of his tripe, the remaining bits of beef stomach in a light red garlic sauce that was an off-menu special at La Manda's each Friday.

As it was bound to, the subject of Paulette's pregnancy came up, along with the fact that she had used "the M word" on two occasions. Johnny voiced his trepidation about the decision he would soon be forced to make, his concern over whether it was wise to tie her down to a much older man, and the likelihood of leaving her a widow with child before she reached her fortieth year.

"I can't advise you on that, my brother. But I will tell you this, that girl is top of the line."

"No doubt about that, man. I think so too."

"You know how I knew she was okay? She never once referred to race, never used the words *black* or *African-American*. I was just plain Pete to her. You know how some white people bring up the subject of race or use the word *African-American*, so you'll think they're on your side?"

"Yeah, now that you mention it. I've noticed that myself."

"It comes off so stilted. You can tell they're not comfortable with it. It's such an unnatural term. Seven syllables where one will do. It sounds so forced, and it makes me feel they're not all that comfortable around me. Not her though. That chick is as natural as they come. Pure fucking class, man. If you want my opinion, you'll never do better than her. Snap her up, dude. She loves her some Johnny Santoro. A girl like that'll stick with you through thick and thin. I'd bet my life on it."

His friend sat there, looking down at his plate, swishing a piece of the fine Italian bread around in what was left of the sauce from his meal, contemplating Pete's words.

That evening, Nicky gave Johnny a pep talk.

"You need to marry that girl, man. Number one, she loves the ground you walk on. Number two, she having your baby and you got to do the right thing by her and your chile."

"Believe me, Nicky, there's nothing I want more than to be with her and be the best daddy I can be to that baby. The question is, do I have the right to tie her up and rob the best years of her life?"

"She done made herself clear on the matter. I don't know why, but it's you she wants, so go for it. Besides, who else gonna want your tired old ass?"

This made Johnny laugh. He could tell Nicky was riding him for his own good.

"Here's something else to think about. This ain't just about her and you. This is the combining of two families, her daddy and his Freemasons plus ours. Bound by blood, the strongest bind there is. I'm tellin' you, boy, I want this. You understand?"

Johnny now saw that his uncle had an agenda that went far beyond just "doing the right thing" for this girl and her baby. This would be a formal blending of two of the most powerful, secret entities in the western world. Was this, he wondered, what Nicky had been after all along? Or, as he'd done his entire life, was he just taking advantage of a situation that fell into his lap?

"Now you get your ass in gear and set a date, and that's all I got to say about it."

"I will, Nicky. I'll do it first thing tomorrow morning."

"Good boy. My wedding gift to you will be a house, wherever you want to live. I wish you all could be down here at home, so I can keep an eye on you and bounce that baby on my knee. But I understand if she wants to be close to her own people. So, I'll leave that up to the two of you. Just make sure you get one big enough for three," he grinned.

"Thank you, Nicky. I wasn't expecting anything so generous."

"You all I got. If I live another hundred years I could never spend all my money, so who else am I gonna give it to? I love you, boy."

"I love you, too, Nicky."

"We'll put it in her name, so when your time comes, there won't be no problems."

They disconnected their iPhones and Johnny went to tell Paulette the news.

CHAPTER 38

CHRISTMAS EVE WAS SPENT WITH HER FAMILY. Cook made her favorite angel food cake with twenty candles on it. What little snow had fallen cleared up by morning. The Gulf Stream kept the Long Island Sound relatively warm through the winter, so there could be a foot of snow inland, west of the Merritt Parkway, and little if any where they lived near the water.

Pierre was down from college in New Haven. He was polite enough, but his time at the family home was limited, as he was pretty serious about a classmate who lived in Rye, another upscale town on the Sound, and spent most of his vacation there with her family. Part of this was due to his continuing discomfort over what had happened to his mother and his inability to face her.

Johnny noticed that he, Michelle and Paulette were not the closest of siblings and were also vastly different personality types. In high school, Pierre would have been deemed a "preppy," and his choices in wardrobe, his Kennedyesque hair style and other affectations reflected this. He was right at home at Yale and was excited at having been told he was a sure thing to be tapped to become a member of Skull and Bones, one of the rare Catholics admitted to membership to that secret society, as had been his father and grandfather.

Many prominent and powerful figures have been members, including former President William Howard Taft and both Bushes, along with numerous governors, Supreme Court Justices and the founder of the CIA. As a Bonesman, Pierre's future could be said to be secure.

As usual, the sullen, monosyllabic Michelle kept to herself, although it didn't appear that she was using drugs at this point. Her parents didn't seem to push her to join in any conversations, indulging her wish to be alone. Johnny observed that she avoided his eyes, leading him to wonder if there'd been any abuse in her background.

Aware that he'd lost everything he owned in the bombing, Patricia had asked him not to buy Christmas presents, which was a relief. Thanks to his insurance settlement, money was no longer an issue; he was just terrible at picking out the right gifts. He didn't trust his taste, and it caused him considerable stress, trying to come up with that certain special item that fit with the personal style of the one for whom he was buying. Especially people like these, who seemingly had everything they could possibly desire, and who possessed a grace and refinement that was beyond anything he had known.

He thought an engagement ring might be something Paulette would like, so he asked her where a good jeweler was and she said she didn't care for engagement rings because they were "a dated custom and a total waste of money." What little jewelry she preferred was simple and tasteful, the kinds of items the average person might not notice. Pieces that did not draw attention to themselves. It was another old money trait of hers. Her clothes were the same, expensive, without looking like they cost a fortune, unless you were from that background. Then you could tell.

She invited him to attend midnight mass with her parents to celebrate both her twentieth birthday and Christmas Eve. The professors at Yale had turned Pierre into an atheist and Michelle just didn't care to leave her room, so they chose to opt out. Their parents had never had the fortitude to press their children to do anything they didn't want to, the result being this unstructured family. Where Paulette learned the self-discipline she possessed was a mystery.

In the afternoon, she asked him to go with her to confession, a sacrament he hadn't received in decades. The thought of it frightened him, but in his desire to please her, he agreed to go.

Founded in 1876, Saint Mary's was one of Greenwich's oldest Roman Catholic churches. Paulette had attended services there with her family her whole life. As an infant, she'd been baptized there, in the sacristy. Johnny sat in the pew and watched as she entered the confessional. Several minutes later, she emerged with her head bowed and knelt beside him to say her penance.

Getting his nerve up, he went in and, on his knees, said the words he somehow managed to recall from his childhood.

"In the name of the Father, the Son and the Holy Ghost."

"I see it's been a while, my son. It's been the Holy *Spirit* for quite a few years now."

"Yes, Father, I guess it has been," he replied, feeling foolish.

"Go ahead, son. Confess your sins."

Nervously, he continued the torture, "Bless me Father, for I have sinned. It's been more than fifty years since my last confession." He paused. "Does it work if I can't remember everything, Father?"

"Just remember what you can."

"I uh, missed Sunday mass all those years. I ate meat on Friday."

The priest smiled and thought to himself, *They always start with the small stuff when they've been away for a long time.* To Johnny, he said, "Eating meat on Friday hasn't been a sin for quite some time either."

"Oh, okay, and I used profanity, took the Lord's name in vain. I masturbated many times and had sexual relations outside of marriage. I uh, I lied. I think I may have stolen, but I'm not sure. I committed adultery."

"Anything else, my son?"

"Yes, Father, something very bad."

"God can forgive anything, son, if you're truly sorry. He loves you and wants you to one day be with Him in Heaven. So, go ahead, don't be afraid. Anything you say here is bound by the seal of the confessional."

He felt as though he might vomit, remembering the sight of Tupac Prentiss's bullet-riddled body and his bloody eyeball on the dirty floor of that hallway, and began to perspire profusely. He felt his bowels growl and feared he might let loose in his trousers at any moment. He gulped and confessed his worst sin, the sin that could condemn him to the fires of hell if he failed to confess it.

"Father, I took part in a murder," he said, adding, "I didn't actually kill the person myself, but I was there and I did nothing to stop it."

"I see. I take it this wasn't in the war. Can you tell me the circumstances under which this sin was committed?"

"I'll try, Father. You see, it was revenge for a woman who was raped. My soon-to-be mother-in-law."

"Murder is a violation of the fifth commandment, *Thou shalt not kill.* 'Revenge is mine, sayeth the Lord.' You understand that it is not our place to extract revenge or to decide another person's punishment. Are you truly sorry for this and all your sins?"

"Yes, Father, I am. I've always tried to be good, but I'm far from perfect."

"You're going to be married soon. Do you think you can be faithful to the young lady?"

"I know I can. I love her." It was the first time he'd spoken those three words aloud, and they struck a chord deep within him. And he knew then and there that he truly did love Paulette.

"Do you remember the story of the prodigal son?"

Johnny nodded as the holy man continued.

"It is a story of redemption, similar to the parable of the lost sheep. God said, 'There is more joy in heaven over one lost sinner who repents and returns to the flock than the other ninety-nine who need no repentance.'

You are the prodigal son and this day, the Lord is joyous because of you, my son."

The priest paused, allowing his words to sink in.

"For your penance, say ten Our Fathers and ten Hail Marys, and make a good Act of Contrition. Go and sin no more. *Ego te absolve a peccatis tuis in nomine Patris, et Filii, et Spiritus Sancti, Amen."*

Tears were now running down his face, for he knew in his heart that he was forgiven. The weight of so many years had been lifted from his shoulders and he felt he was now possibly worthy of the gift of Paulette's love and that of the child she carried in her womb.

He went to the communion rail before the altar and knelt on the cold tiles to say his penance. With the fresh, clear eyes of one forgiven, he could now see that the church was really quite beautiful. There were arches on either side of the pews, past which he could see the stained-glass windows containing tableaus of various biblical events. The dome high above the altar was as perfectly blue as the sky and dotted with tiny, illuminated bulbs that represented the stars in the heavens. He imagined how the pipes of the ancient organ in the balcony in the back of the church must sound playing the eerie Gregorian chants. He now felt absolved of his sins and in a state of holy grace.

When he'd finished praying, he stood up and Paulette joined him and took his arm as they walked up the aisle and out to where the car was parked.

"I'm so happy you did that for me, baby," she said. "Now we can start our life together with a clean slate. Thank you so much. I know it wasn't easy."

CHAPTER 39

BACK IN WASHINGTON NOW, TONY WAS STILL
wondering if what he'd seen flying on the starboard side of Air Force Two
was real or had he dreamt it. A lifelong pragmatist, he wasn't the type given
to wasting his time thinking about things he could not prove. But here was
something he'd seen with his own eyes. Or had he?

Whichever, he was unable to erase that visual from his mind, and so he
went about checking to see just who might be able to fill him in on whether
there were in fact extraterrestrial beings, and whether they were in contact
with earthlings and, more specifically, American earthlings.

He went into the president's office and asked whether he'd been filled
in more completely on the subject yet. Tony had been around Washington
long enough to have heard the rumors that every president since at least
Eisenhower had had contact with an advanced alien civilization, but so
far, the Rock had been told nothing for certain and, in the excitement
of his first days in office, hadn't thought to ask. In truth, the subject had
never crossed his mind before. As Nicky had mentioned, anyone could
google "Clinton/aliens" and read how the randy ex-president had been
on the verge of revealing the supposed existence of these beings when the
brouhaha over his impeachment diverted his, and the public's, attention.

Tony had his assistant track down former South Carolina Senator
Ernest "Fritz" Hollings, who was pushing one hundred years old. They'd

known each other in the Senate and played ball with each other on votes for various bills over the years, during that lost era when the parties still believed in the axiom that "One hand washes the other."

"Fritz, baby, how you been?"

"Oh, as well as can be expected at my age. Speak up, will you? My hearing's not what it once was. Congratulations on the election, boy. What can I do for you?"

"Listen, I'm on my private line, so we can talk. I been hearing for years them stories about contact between our leaders and beings from other planets, but so far, nobody's mentioned anything definite to either me or the president. What can you tell me?"

"Well, that stuff's a little outside my wheelhouse, son, but I can tell you this, the people to talk to are not NASA. However, if you have anybody close to you at Intelligence...."

His tired old mind drifted off at that point and he started talking football, so Tony bid him good-bye and thought about who he knew at the higher levels of the intelligence community that he could trust with these kinds of questions. There was one fellow, a four-star general. He wasn't at the very top level, but he would know who to speak to. For our purposes here, we'll call him "X,"

Contact with X was made on Tony's behalf and a meeting was set at a discrete location, the former estate of abolitionist Frederick Douglass at 1411 W Street SE in Cedar Hill, near the Anacostia River. Tony's Secret Service contingent drove him there and one of the agents checked inside the house and then both waited on the porch out front while the vice-president and X met in private.

The gentleman we're calling X was a man in his mid-80s, still quite spry and alert. He began by saying, "You realize that anything said on this subject is top secret and cannot be revealed."

Tony nodded and X continued, "As far as we know, General Eisenhower met with Winston Churchill during the latter part of the war to discuss an encounter by an RAF reconnaissance aircraft with a UFO near the western English coastline. In that meeting, Churchill reportedly told Ike, 'This event should be immediately classified, as it would create mass panic amongst the general population and destroy one's belief in the Church.'"

"I always been a fan of Churchill. I think he's the greatest man of the 20th century," said Tony.

"Yes, well anyway, he felt belief in God was important for the morale of his people. Remember, at the time, London was being bombarded by the German *Luftwaffe*. FDR made some cryptic remarks hinting at the subject publicly, and Truman later shut down public knowledge about the Roswell crash in 1947 and what they found there, but we have no solid evidence that either of them had actual contact, in the sense that words were exchanged."

"I liked ol' Harry too. He had to make some tough ass decisions."

"Kennedy wanted to go public and demanded the CIA hand over secret files on the subject, but, with his growing reliance on pain-killing drugs, it was felt he couldn't be trusted to keep quiet. Times when the drugs took hold, he even talked about sharing alien technology with the Soviets, for Christ's sake. Nixon had tried to have a documentary made using secret footage of an alien craft, but that idea was shot down by Intelligence. The fool wanted something that would ensure his place in history."

"Can you tell me if any presidents actually had personal, face-to-face contact with aliens? Besides Eisenhower, I mean."

"Eisenhower had three such meetings in 1954 at Holloman Air Force base in New Mexico. Bush senior, of course knew, as does W. I personally am not aware if other presidents have been in contact, but I suspect they may have. Trump liked to hint about having had contact, but he was full of shit and liked to brag about things that made him feel important. It is highly unlikely that ETs would have had any interest in speaking with either him or President Silverman."

"Is there a possibility that I might look at some of the files?"

"That would be the president's call, sir, assuming the top people in my section would agree. Let me speak to them and get back to you."

"One more thing. Wernher von Braun. Did he get his knowledge about rockets from them?" His mind was running wild now. "And what about that reverse engineering? And if so, do we know why they approached and helped the Nazis before us?"

"That, sir, is a question for the ages," and he offered nothing more.

Tony thanked him for his time and went out to the SUV with his security detail and back to the White House to try and put all this together. In the back of his mind, a thought was starting to form that, should these extraterrestrials exist, and should they believe America was the best choice to survive, how could they be used to defeat a Fourth Reich eager for our destruction, and located in our very own hemisphere?

CHAPTER 40

WHEN HE RETURNED TO THE WHITE HOUSE, TONY told the president about his conversation with X and filled him in on his suspicions regarding the rise of a Nazi movement in Paraguay and the possibility that they may have been behind the bombing of Los Angeles.

"Wow, this is some far out stuff," said the Rock. "Should I meet with this guy? And where do we go from there?"

Suddenly realizing that others might be listening, and that he might have already said too much, Tony answered carefully, "On something like this, before we make a move, I might need to talk to somebody first," by which he meant Nicky. "I'll get back to you."

His security guys took him to the house that had been rented for him for the duration of his term, where he pressed the "on" button on the video game he'd purchased for the purpose of his private, encrypted conversations with Nicky. Now fearful of possible bugs in the house, he turned on some loud music and spoke softly into the game's mic. Then he put on his earphones.

"Okay, I talked with this cat in Intelligence. He was pretty cagey, but, without coming out and saying, he pretty much confirmed that other presidents have had contact and, at least at one time they was on our side."

"Good, now you gotta get the Rock to put him and you in touch with these things, or whatever they are. You need to lay it all out for them, how the Germans are fixin' to start up a Fourth Reich and how they bombed LA, and all that shit. Find out if they'll help. Remind them they helped us in World War II, then let me know how it goes."

They disconnected and Nicky sat back in his chair, and his mind drifted off to simpler times and simpler problems, like when he was a kid before the war and the hardest thing in his day was to figure out how to pass the counterfeit tens and twenties Carlos had given him to put out on the street.

"Man, those was the fun days," he told young Ned, who was all ears. "I was living in the Quarter then. Sam Butera was twelve, already playin' a hell of a saxophone. I'd bring him to the after hours joints with Louis Prima's brother, Leon and he'd play with the colored musicians and knock 'em right outta their sox. I was seventeen and already runnin' three or four whores. Makin' pretty good money. Carlos would give me a paper bag with five thousand in counterfeit bills to spread around."

"How'd you get away with that, Nicky?"

"Shit, boy, Carlos was king 'round here. Who was gonna say no to me, who was workin' for him? I remember one time they printed up a bad batch. They was yellow, like real obvious, and I tried to pass 'em in a bank over the state line in Nacogdoches in East Texas. The teller looked at the bills and said, 'I'm sorry young man, but we can't accept these. They're not real and I have to confiscate them.' She called the manager, who tried to get all big and bad with me, saying, 'Who gave you this money, kid? You can go to jail if you don't tell.' Shit, that woulda been a Federal rap, crossin' state lines."

"Geez, what did you do?"

"I told him I couldn't tell. Then he called the sheriff and he tried to get tough with me, sayin' 'If you don't tell, I'm gonna lock you up and beat your dago ass until you tell me.'"

"Were you scared?"

"He was a big, fat fuck, with a cowboy hat and big cigar in his fat fucking mouth. He slapped me in my face and I wanted to stick him with my knife, but I stayed cool and asked if he ever heard the name Carlos Marcello."

Nicky laughed at the memory and went on, "Oh man, you shoulda seen. That fat bastard started to cry like a mother fuckin' girl. He said, 'Oh please, please don't tell Mr. Carlos. We'll take the money. Please.' I thought he was gonna pee his pants. Ah, man, them was the fun days." He laughed so hard, he began to cough.

He rang the kitchen for some sandwiches and beverages.

"Hey Carmine, make me a sandwich with *capicol'*, *mortadell'* and *provalone*. What you want, kid?"

"I'll have whatever you're having."

"Make him the same thing and bring us a couple-a ginger ales."

Ned wanted an RC Cola, but was too shy to ask.

Nicky then told him what he'd learned from his conversation with Tony.

"Now if we can get these space people to listen, Tony will explain that the Nazis might start some shit that could wind up destroying the whole world. Tell 'em they need to take out the leaders or show us how to do it. That's the plan, plain and simple. They must have some reason why they helped us in the past, something that might mean earth is important to them somehow. Something they need here. Or that they got some stake in America succeeding. Remember, kid, you always gotta consider what's in it for the other guy. That's true all over the universe, wherever you go."

Ned listened intently, as if he were being handed the wisdom of the gods from some shaman.

"So, you see, what I need from you could save the world, young man. Do you understand what I'm telling you?"

"Yes sir, I do."

"You need to find out exactly who and where them Nazi leaders are, as close as you can. Then, the CIA or whoever can go down there and make sure, so the aliens or our guys can do the do. Who knows? Maybe the aliens already know where they are and all Tony has to do is figure out what they want and make a deal with 'em. That man could sell snow to Eskimos. This shit is way over my head too, kid, so I don't expect you to get it all either. Just do everything I tell you."

CHAPTER 41

X'S SUPERIOR, WHO WE SHALL REFER TO AS "Y," WAS well aware of the obstacles involved when Tony informed him of the likelihood of Nazis in South America being behind the LA bombing.

"As I see it," Tony began, "there's no other way. We can't just go in there and bomb the hell out of them. What would it make us look like?"

"No question. We'd be portrayed as colonialists, attempting to annex the entire southern hemisphere. That could set off things with China or Russia or both."

"That's what I'm saying, man."

"There's one other thing to consider. If the ETs' involvement gets out, the plan for revelation will be pushed far in advance of the public being prepared to hear of it. Our time line, up to now, has been for disclosure to occur in roughly five more years. If we let it out too soon, there's the risk of mass hysteria and world-wide panic."

"I get it, but how long before these Nazis hit us with another big one? Talk about risk. Can we risk losing New York? Washington? You wanna talk about some panic. That'll be some panic for your ass."

"Let me discuss it with my people, Mr. Vice-President, uh, and you too, Mr. President." It was now clear to Tony that word was already out in the Capitol that he, not President Johnson, was the man in charge.

On the drive back in the president's car, called Cadillac One, Limousine One or, colloquially, the Beast, they rolled up the window between the driver and themselves so they could speak.

"Thank God you were there, Tony. I'm so way over my head, I'm freaking out."

"Stay calm, good buddy. You gonna be okay. Me and Nicky got this. When the cat from Intelligence gets back to me, tonight or tomorrow, I'll sound you and, hopefully, we'll get a meet with these space dudes and work something out. Just be cool, Daddy-O."

Later that night, a little before midnight, the call came from Y. A meeting had been arranged for the president and himself at the location known as Area 51, near Edwards Air Force Base, some 83 miles north-northwest of Las Vegas, Nevada.

"Great, when is it for?"

"Immediately, Sir. Air Force One is being fueled as we speak and your security team is waiting outside your house now."

"I'll be ready in five. Have you spoke to the president?"

"Yes Sir, he's getting dressed. I and an associate will be flying out with you as well. Oh, and the "others" have been made aware that they'll be dealing mainly with you."

Quickly, Tony fired up the video game. He'd chosen *Lara Croft: Tomb Raider*, because he had the hots for Angelina Jolie, in her younger incarnation. How many times had he gotten his rocks off watching the ravishing cartoon version of her, shooting and killing bad guys?

"Nicky, it's on. Me and the Rock are flying off to meet them now."

"Okay, baby. This is your big moment. Just keep your cool. I know you can handle this. May the mother fucking Force be with your ass," they both tried to laugh but, in truth, Tony was shitting in his pants.

CHAPTER 42

ALL DURING THE FLIGHT THERE, BOTH MEN SAT in a nervous silence, broken only by the occasional instructions and advice from Y and the agents and scientists who accompanied them.

Why can't he be the same heroic Rock like in the movies? The guy who always saves the day? thought Tony.

"Don't be put off by their voices, which will sound somewhat odd to human ears. They have the ability to speak and understand all our languages. We don't know for sure whether they have telepathic powers, but we think they do. So, insofar far as you're able, be careful of your thoughts. Another thing, they appear to have no sense of humor, so no jokes or wisecracks please."

"Reminds me of my first wife," cracked the president. No one laughed.

Roughly five and a half hours later, they landed and four military vehicles took them to a large hangar where, once inside, their eyes grew wide at the sight of a large disc-shaped object. Tony judged it to be approximately forty feet in diameter, with what looked like hieroglyphics on its dull, metallic surface. There was an opening underneath with a bright light that shown down from the interior.

"The way it works is, you stand in the light, one at a time and you'll be loaded up into the craft. Good luck, gentlemen."

From someplace inside himself, maybe he was in character and a better actor than anyone had taken him for, but the president assumed the role of a movie hero and walked confidently into the light, whereupon he was sucked up inside. Not to be upstaged, Tony followed suit and they soon found themselves looking at five or six creatures.

They look just like in the fucking movies, Tony thought, as he regarded these small gray beings, maybe four feet tall, with large, elongated heads and impossibly huge eyes, little holes for ears and for breathing, and small mouths with no lips. They wore no clothing and he could see no genitalia between their legs. *They fingers is longer than Chuck Berry's,* he thought to himself.

"Your New Orleans dialect is quite charming, Tony," came the oddest voice he'd ever heard from one of the creatures. "If I may call you by your first name. I mean no disrespect."

"How'd you do that?" Tony asked.

"You would call it telepathy. We can communicate in silence or by speaking out loud, whichever you prefer. I suspect you're more used to using your voice."

He was beginning to feel more comfortable now. He wasn't sure if it was the creature's gentle, relaxed demeanor or it was a kind of mind control putting him at ease.

"I do have the ability to control or change your thoughts and feelings, Tony, but I am not doing so at the moment. We come as friends, to use a word you're familiar with."

"I'm not used to people reading my mind, so let me apologize in advance if anything I think might offend you."

"The word *offense* is not in our lexicon. It's not an emotion we feel. In fact, your concepts of emotion are unknown to us. It's one of many traits that have been bred out of us over many thousands of years as useless and unproductive. Long, long ago, our ancestors looked not unlike you, with fur like yours on our heads and bodies, and genitals that were there for all to see. Our planet has a temperature that never changes; it is perfectly comfortable, day or night, so there is no need for clothing. But you're not here for a lesson on who we are. You have need of our knowledge and skills, so may we discuss your needs at this time?"

The president stood there in awe, unable to speak. The beings understood this and projected thoughts and visions into his mind designed to bring him comfort and ease. They seemed to intuit that Tony was the alpha between the two of them, despite the Rock's higher title.

Tony tried to block a thought but could not. *I wonder who's the male and who's the female and how they tell each other apart? They got no dicks or pussies.*

"That's an understandable question, Tony," said the one who was doing all the talking. "Over the course of our evolution, the concept of male and female became important only insofar as procreation is concerned. When that becomes necessary, we have a process by which our genitalia emerge and, as you would say, do their job. Do we enjoy it, you're asking yourself? Yes, we do, very much."

A sexually curious man, now Tony was interested in hearing more.

The being, sensing his interest, went on, seeming to enjoy seeing him titillated. "I hope this isn't too much information for you to take in so early in our friendship, but many thousands of years ago, we visited your planet and found what we needed to save our own from destruction. It was gold, a necessary component in our devices, but we needed physical help in mining it, so we experimented with combining our DNA with that of the upright creatures we found living here. And you, dear friend, are the end result."

He wondered whether they did this combining in test tubes or actually had sex with the earthlings, and he found himself becoming aroused.

"We experimented both ways," the being answered his thought, now enjoying Tony's discomfort even more. "You must have read about the gods who coupled with earthlings in your school textbooks on ancient

Greece. Did you think these were simply myths? Did it never occur to you that these "myths" were true accounts of actual occurrences? I can read in your memory bank that, as a young boy, these stories aroused you, just as you are aroused now."

He was frightened and turned on at the same time.

"You're wondering whether I am male or female. In our world, neither male nor female has the greater power or authority, and our maleness or femaleness only emerges when it's time for coitus. And, like you, we engage in coitus for pleasure, although we have no moral constraints barring us from copulating with whomever we are attracted to. Our only rule regarding sex is that it must be consensual. This is something we are extremely strict about. The punishment for non-consensual intercourse is death."

He thought he saw what looked like a smile forming on the being's face.

"To answer the questions in your mind, Tony, I am female, and I am what you'd call the commander of this craft. Perhaps you'd like to continue this conversation alone with me."

Good grief, is she coming on to me? Was she controlling his mind? Did she possess the power to control his libido too? All he knew was, he hadn't felt so turned on in years.

One of the other beings placed the tips of two long fingers over the president's eyes and instantly he was out cold in a hypnotic trance. The one who'd done all the talking took Tony's hand in hers and led him to another room and ordered him to remove his clothing and, not knowing why or how, he obeyed without question. From between her short legs, a human-like vagina appeared and, in moments, she was upon him.

The sex was frighteningly intense and, he had to admit, amazing, somehow endowing him with the powers he'd had as a younger man. Her tongue was some six inches long and it practically choked him when she kissed him. When it was over, she warned him, "Earth men tend to feel differently about their partner after climaxing. Rather than see you with feelings of regret or shame, if you wish, I can erase all memory of what just happened or I can give you a remembrance that will be pleasing whenever you think of me."

"Uh, how was it for you?" he asked, out of habit, immediately feeling stupid for using such a corny cliché. "I meant…ah shit, I don't even know what I meant."

She caressed his face with her long fingers and said, "I think I shall allow you a pleasant memory of this erotic experience," and, as one presses the "send" button on an email, that picture went straight to his memory bank. "Interspecies intercourse is common practice with us. I'd hate to leave you with feelings of guilt over what happened between us. As I said earlier, such emotions are unknown to us, although pleasure is not. To answer your question, I found you quite enjoyable. Now, shall we return to the others and discuss your more immediate needs?"

Back in the main "cabin," if you will, what appeared to be an assistant brought the president out of his hypnotic state and they discussed America's problem with the bombing and the Nazis, and what might be done about it.

"To answer your first question, these Nazis in South America were indeed responsible for the destruction of your city. As for a curative, there are any number of scenarios. This group's ancestors gave you trouble some years ago. You won the conflict and they seem to have an irrational, childish desire for revenge. We could erase that need in them. Or we could destroy them or give you the means to do so yourselves, either quickly or over a longer period of time, which would be helpful to your nation's economy, but cost you the lives of many brave young soldiers. The opposite side of that coin is that war often brings a nation together, something your country has needed for many years. However, Mr. President, your unprecedented popularity can go a long way toward remedying that. But to accomplish this, you need to stay alive. The possibilities, you see, are virtually endless, limited only by the imagination and what you and your people have the stomach for."

"Can you help us decide?" the Rock suddenly spoke for the first time since they'd arrived.

"I perceive you as a kind-hearted man, Mr. President. You didn't really seek this job, did you?"

"Honestly, no, I didn't. And I'm finding that the pressure is too much for me."

"Worse than making your moving pictures, yes? We feel you are not cut out for this kind of pressure. You also have a weak heart, despite your powerful looking physique. I should warn you, if you do not learn to relax, you are unquestionably on the road to a heart attack. To protect you from this danger, we will place in your mind all the information you need to know how to take care of your health. You must follow these instructions to the letter if you wish to live out the term of your presidency. And living out your term is, we believe, something that would be good for your country."

The Rock, suddenly filled with the knowledge that what he was being told about his health was the gods' honest truth, thanked his new extra-terrestrial friend. He was now fully conscious of which holistic medications, exercise regimens and diet would save his life and was determined to follow them religiously in the future.

"Seeing first hand, what we are able to do, I suspect you have a pretty good idea of how you want to handle your Nazi problem."

"Tony, will you please take this one," said the president.

"Yes sir, Mr. President. I think the best solution is for you folks to soften their minds and hearts toward us. There's been too much bloodshed, and too much discord."

"You are a wise man Mr. Vice President, and you've made the right decision, not only for your country, but for your planet. You will come to see how the right choice in the right moment can be best for everyone."

She looked around the room, apparently communicating silently with the others, and then, "I do believe we've reached the end of our meeting.

Thank you for coming. It's been a great pleasure," then, looking slyly at Tony, she said, "in more ways than one."

"We are eternally grateful for your help," he replied.

"Oh, and Tony, please give my regards to your friend, Mr. Santoro in New Orleans and tell him I may stop by and surprise him one day in the near future."

Tony looked at her, not comprehending.

"Think about it, Tony. Have you never awakened from a pleasurable dream that seemed more real than reality? One you feared might possibly have been real? Well, even old men have such dreams."

And, just like that, he and the Rock were gently transported back to the floor of the hangar. From a small office in the building, the officials, scientists and medical doctors emerged to greet them. Once they all had stepped away from the ship, it took off silently and with incredible speed, disappearing from sight in seconds.

Tony and the president were driven to the base medical center and examined by the doctors, who found them to be in better physical condition than before. The nurse who hung up Tony's clothing during the examination noticed semen stains on his underwear but said nothing to anyone. Not ever.

CHAPTER 43

JANUARY 6TH, THE FEAST OF THE EPIPHANY, marked the visit of the three wise men, the Magi, to the baby Jesus, bringing Him gifts of gold, frankincense and myrrh. It is said to be the date of His baptism. It was also the date Paulette chose as the date for her wedding to Johnny Santoro.

Her mother's wedding gown fit her perfectly, as Patricia had also been pregnant on her own wedding day. The dress was the traditional something old. The something new was the simple, antique cross Johnny had given her. For something borrowed, she wore an old silver charm bracelet loaned to her by Betty. Her something blue was a royal blue ribbon that Michelle tied around her other wrist.

With her hair done up in the tight French twist redolent of Catherine Deneuve's, she looked as beautiful as any bride anyone in Greenwich had ever seen. Her happiness was contagious, so much so that not one snide remark was made, or even considered, throughout the ceremony.

Pete was his friend's best man. He did not forget the ring and they both looked handsome in their tuxedos. Michelle, too old to be a flower girl and too young to be the bride's maid, saw service holding the train of her sister's gown as she walked down the aisle to the traditional strains of Richard Wagner's "Bridal Chorus." Carole Holman served as bride's maid.

St. Mary's was adorned with flowers, the largest and most beautiful arrangement sent by Nicky, followed in size only by those from Vito Gennaro and Tony Calabrese, whose card read "To Mr. & Mrs. Johnny Santoro. Best of everything from the Vice President of the United States," along with a letter of congratulations from the president himself on White House stationary. The card that came with Nicky's flowers read, "All happiness to my loyal nephew and his beautiful bride on your happy day." The church was filled to capacity and the choir sang beautifully.

For reasons known only to herself, Patricia cried when the happy couple kissed after saying "I do." Following the kiss, the bride and groom exited to Felix Mendelssohn's "Wedding March."

The reception was held immediately afterwards at Greenwich Country Club. Nicky had two bands flown up, one that played traditional New Orleans jazz of the Louis Armstrong and Jelly Roll Morton school for the older folks, and Irma Thomas and her band for the younger people to dance to. Ms. Thomas did *not* sing "You Can Have My Husband." Everyone had a good time and the party was the talk of Greenwich for the next few months.

Now man and wife, it was time to look for a home of their own. To give Paulette some rest, two days later, Johnny kept an appointment with a real estate broker who showed him several houses in a price range he felt was respectful to Nicky's generosity, all of which were very nice, but not quite right.

After lunch, he found one in North White Plains that had the right feel he was sure she would like and he called to see if she felt up to taking a look that afternoon. She said she'd noticed some spotting and was feeling a bit tired and would it be all right to put it off until morning. He said he'd be right over to take her to the doctor's but she said her mother had already done so and everything turned out to be fine.

"Baby, I'll be napping, so why don't you go hang out at Pete's the rest of the afternoon. It's such a nice day out." Before hanging up, she said "I love you so much my darling husband. Please, never ever forget that. I promise I will love you forever and a day, and to the stars and back." There was something in the way she said it that gave him a strange, almost ominous feeling.

It was, in fact, an unseasonably warm day, a record-breaking seventy-one degrees, unheard of for January. So, he thought he'd take a ride by himself up to the Kensico Dam, the place where they fell in love.

He parked in the same spot, on the west side of the reservoir, and walked up to the roadway where they'd stood together that day. He looked out onto the water where he saw one small boat containing an old, white bearded man wearing a wide-brimmed straw hat who was fishing near the wooded island in the middle of the lake. He stood there and watched, thinking he was the luckiest man in the world. He thought of the old Jackie Wilson song, "To Be Loved," recalling Jackie's soulful voice, and how it cracked in melisma when he sang the lyrics, *Oh, what a feeling, to be loved.* And he was happy, happier than he'd ever thought possible.

He turned to his right and saw a woman some distance from where he stood on the roadway. As she advanced toward him, he saw she was beautiful, blonde like his wife. "My wife," he smiled as he said the words out loud, "My beautiful wife who loves me so."

The woman drew nearer. From a distance, she resembled Paulette somewhat, but as she neared, she appeared more like his mother, or as he imagined her at Paulette's age.

"*Gianni,*" he thought he heard her say. "*Gianni cara, sono io, Mama.*"

"Excuse me, what did you say?"

"Johnny darling, it's me, Mama."

No, he thought. *This can't be. Am I losing my mind?*

She wore a flowing white dress and as she approached him, reached out and touched his cheek with her soft hand. "I've come for you Johnny. Don't be afraid. I'm here with you now."

"No Mama, I have to go home, to my wife. I have a beautiful wife now. You'll love her."

"I already love her. I knew you loved each other *nel momento in cui e successo.*"

"What do you mean, 'the moment it happened?' The moment what happened? We've been together since September, when the bomb dropped and the electrical grid went down."

"Honey, there was no bomb. There was no grid that went down."

"But her mom was raped and we went after the ones who did it. Uncle Nicky helped too."

"No sweetheart. None of that happened."

"Yes, Uncle Nicky set it up for us with Vito. He made Tony Calabrese vice president. There were Nazis…and aliens."

"*Ascoltami Gianni.* Listen to me. Nicky did nothing of the kind. None of that was real."

"Mama! What's going on? What are you saying? I remember it all so clearly. I came out of the shower. I had the towel wrapped around me and…"

Tears were now flowing down his face. She smiled at him lovingly.

"And nothing, my sweet boy. That was the moment. You fell. Your poor heart gave out. Paulette screamed. She knelt beside you and held you in her arms. She told you she would love you forever and a day and to the stars and back if you just please don't die. But it was too late; you were already gone. The poor thing, she cried for days afterwards."

"No Mama, please, no!"

"A month later, her period didn't come and the next month it failed to come again. She vowed to have that baby. *Il tuo bambina piccola.* She's going to be a loving mother and she'll make sure your little girl never forgets her papa. Her name is Colette."

"Am I dead?"

"Yes, my love. But there is no time in this place where we're going, so you'll see her again one day soon and be together again. *Sempre e per sempre.* Forever and always. Like I told you when you were a little boy, you must always believe in true love, for true love is forever, *il vero amore e per sempre*. You'll be with us always. It's so beautiful here. You'll see."

He was dumbfounded. He had no words.

"You remember how people used to say your life flashes before your eyes at the moment of transition? Well it's not exactly like that. The time in between is like a dream, in your case a crazy, crazy dream, eh?

"Yeah Ma, a real crazy dream, but with a happy ending."

He smiled at her.

"Yes, baby, a happy ending. Come, take my hand."

The man in the boat was drawing closer now and Johnny understood that he was coming to take them. To the beautiful place.

Home.